AF539019

Pure Sequence

Author of more than nineteen books, **Paro Anand** is a performance storyteller and runs a programme, Literature in Action. She has worked with children in difficult circumstances including the orphans of Kashmir and children of poachers in Madhya Pradesh. A record holder for making the world's longest newspaper with children, she has been awarded for contribution to children's literature by President Abdul Kalam and the Russian Centre for Science and Culture. Her novel *No Guns At My Son's Funeral* was nominated onto the IBBY Honor List, 2006, as the best book for young people from India. It is translated into Spanish and German.

Paro was writer-in-residence at the Woodstock School, Mussoorie, where she wrote this first novel for adults, a book celebrating the grace and strength of older women.

BOOKS BY THE SAME AUTHOR

Paro Anand	*I'm Not Butter Chicken*
Paro Anand	*Wingless*
Paro Anand	*Weed*
Paro Anand	*No Guns at My Son's Funeral*

OTHER INDIAINK TITLES

Anjana Basu	*Black Tongue*
Anjana Basu	*Chinku and the Wolfboy*
Anjum Hasan	*Neti, Neti*
A.N.D. Haksar	*Madhav & Kama: A Love Story from Ancient India*
Boman Desai	*Servant, Master, Mistress*
C.P. Surendran	*An Iron Harvest*
Haider Warraich	*Auras of the Jinn*
I. Allan Sealy	*The Everest Hotel*
I. Allan Sealy	*Trotternama*
Indrajit Hazra	*The Garden of Earthly Delights*
Jaspreet Singh	*17 Tomatoes: Tales from Kashmir*
Jawahara Saidullah	*The Burden of Foreknowledge*
John MacLithon	*Hindutva, Sex & Adventure*
Kalpana Swaminathan	*The Page 3 Murders*
Kalpana Swaminathan	*The Gardener's Song*
Kamalini Sengupta	*The Top of the Raintree*
Madhavan Kutty	*The Village Before Time*
Pankaj Mishra	*The Romantics*
Rakesh Satyal	*Blue Boy*
Ranjit Lal	*The Life & Times of Altu-Faltu*
Ranjit Lal	*The Small Tigers of Shergarh*
Ranjit Lal	*The Simians of South Block and Yumyum Piglets*
Raza Mir & Ali Husain Mir	*Anthems of Resistance: A Celebration of Progressive Urdu Poetry*
Sanjay Bahadur	*The Sound of Water*
Shandana Minhas	*Tunnel Vision*
Selina Sen	*A Mirror Greens in Spring*
Sharmistha Mohanty	*New Life*
Shree Ghatage	*Brahma's Dream*
Sudhir Thapliyal	*Crossing the Road*
Susan Visvanathan	*Something Barely Remembered*
Susan Visvanathan	*The Visiting Moon*
Susan Visvanathan	*The Seine at Noon*
Tushar Raheja	*Run Romi Run*

FORTHCOMING TITLES

Ranjit Lal	*Black Limericks*
Tanushree Podder	*Escape from Harem*

Pure Sequence

The story of growing old gracefully or otherwise

Paro Anand

IndiaInk
ROLI BOOKS

© Paro Anand, 2011

All rights reserved. No part of the publication may be reproduced or transmitted, in any form or by any means, without the prior permission of the publisher.

All characters and events in this book are fictitious and any resemblance to real characters, living or dead is purely coincidental.

First published in 2011
IndiaInk
An imprint of
Roli Books Pvt Ltd
M-75, Greater Kailash II Market
New Delhi 110 048
Phone: ++91 (011) 4068 2000
Fax: ++91 (011) 2921 7185
E-mail: info@rolibooks.com; Website: www.rolibooks.com

Also at
Bangalore, Chennai, Jaipur & Mumbai

ISBN: 978-81-86939-56-7

Typeset in Adobe Jenson Pro by Roli Books Pvt Ltd
and printed at Excel Printers, Delhi.

Acknowledgements

In grateful acknowledgement to the Woodstock School, Mussoorie, who gave me a beautiful cottage and a generous writer in residency where the story finally took shape. And to Steve Alter, thank you for all the care, company and food you provided during my stay at Woodstock.

Thank you to all the beautiful women who have brought colour into my life – to Ma, Mummy, Toshi Masi – my six month mother, Nano – aunt and friend, Usha Masi – the undaunted spirit, and so many others.

To my daughter Aditi, whose laughter fills my life. To Uday, my sukoon, special thanks for the title and all the help. To Keshav my beloved best friend and pillar, for never letting me get away with less. Thank you all for helping me grow up and write my first novel for adults! And then, in grateful acknowledgement of Bindiya Thapar – soul sister and pillar of many strengths, whose whimsy and elegance finally gave us the cover we all loved.

3 September 2010 Paro Anand
New Delhi

To
Toshi Masi and Nani,
the funnest women ever,
wish you could have seen this

1

The click of counters, the clink of cup on saucer, the crunch of dentures on biscuits, the snap of shuffled cards, the bids: those were the old lady sounds that emanated once a week from this ensemble of four.

'Declared,' smiled Satya.

'Hai, hai, I've got a full hand.'

'Free hand with a paplu for me!'

'I have a rotten full hand ...,' Kunti muttered. 'Assee, nabey, poorey sau ... you've lost a full hundred points, Kunti,' said Satya, totting up everyone's points on the score sheet she always kept. Satya had been a Math teacher all her life; until very recently; hence she was always entrusted with keeping scores.

'Hai Satya, the luck is really running with you today, lucky yaar!'

'Too good, you dealt me a six-card pure sequence, I got too excited looking at my lucky hand,' Satya laughed.

'Don't forget what they say, lucky in cards ... unlucky in ....'

'Love,' they all chorused. It was a word they loved to say, especially in chorus. Out loud. For it wasn't a word that one boldly mouthed on one's own. Especially not at 'our age'! They uttered the word as often as possible, on any excuse, for each one felt – in her own way – she didn't have as much love in her life as the others had.

Truth be told, they weren't far off the mark. Love was not an over-the-counter commodity for them in these autumnal years. Love flowed downwards now from them to others, whoever the others might be. It was different for each of them – an ill, almost-on-his-death-bed-for-seven-years husband in the case of Sheila Satija; grandchildren in the cases of Tosh Bhatia who couldn't have enough of them and Kunti Chadda who had altogether had too much of hers. But love was probably the rarest commodity for Satya Kapoor: a spinster in her little DDA MIG flat bought out of a teacher's salary scraped together over forty years.

'Kyun unlucky kehtey ho apney aap ko Satya, you're not unlucky. In fact, you're really lucky to be your own master, do as you like, when you like, how you like.'

'Yes, not like me, hai na Tosh? You'll agree, my life toh is full of fighting, fighting, fighting.'

'Arrey, at least you have people to fight with, all *I* fight is loneliness ...,' Satya's voice broke, edged with tears.

'And your doodhwala? And your part-time woman? Don't forget them, you fight with them all the time!' The other three women burst out laughing.

'Hain, hain, make fun of me, I'm used to it. First it was the school-children who used to make fun of my saris and my English pronounciation, now you ... theek hai, mazaak ura lo ... after all, I'm just a washed out yellow.' This last was muttered low, not meant for the others to hear. Perhaps she hadn't really said it out loud. Satya often saw people in colours. She had assigned each of her friends a colour. She never shared this with the others, knowing that they would laugh at her whimsical ways. She herself was a pale yellow. Sometimes pretty, in a soft way, but most often pasty and too pale to be really noticeable. Mostly a DDA yellow.

Sheila Satija (a leafy green, like new leaves) was used to mothering adults and soothing cranky tantrums and she quickly poured a soothing cup of elaichi tea, 'Relax, Satya, it's okay: just a joke ....'

'How come the joke's always on me, huh, you tell me that?'

'Accha, accha, sorry, bhai,' said Kunti, who had started it all, 'chalo ji, whose deal is it?'

'Sheila, your deal, let's get on with the game.'

Sheila Satija had been nursing her husband for the past seven years, after he was paralyzed by a massive stroke. His speech, his movement, even his brain had been robbed by the stroke. Now he lay in bed drooling and moaning. In fact, she was always the stronger of the two, often doing the more physical of jobs. But he had been no shirker either. They would both take on a great deal of physical labour, even managing their large garden all by themselves and getting a part-time mali to come and do some occasional hedge-pruning and the like. Now of course, because of his condition, the workload was a lot more and a male nurse came in the mornings to help her with the heavy work like bathing him and changing his sheets and clothes. But after that Sheila was all alone the whole day. She had a maid, a good one who had been with her for twelve years, but her husband wouldn't let the maid touch him. He wanted his wife by his side. And he wanted her all the time. The hours passed by in a set rhythm of duties. The humdrum roll of making khichdi, hand grinding it to a paste, mixing in a little sweetened curd, soft but not soupy; the water in his plastic sipper had to be just right, lukewarm, not hot nor cold. Then the tying of the bib, cajoling him eat, little games to get him to open his mouth – 'dekho, plane aa raha hai, kaun aya plane mein – dekho, bhai sahab bethey hain, jaldi sey muh kholo taki plane land kar jaye!' Yes, he had regressed and she pampered him like a mother, not like a wife. And the love flowed downwards now. Downwards and one way. For he was mostly cranky and only complained. Never once would he say, 'Sheila, meri jaan, how good you are to me, looking after my every need. What did I do to deserve a wife like you?'

Sheila Satija enjoyed it in one way. The physicality of the work gave her day a backbone. It made her feel strong and whole as though she hadn't aged at all. It made her feel needed. Since Annu – their daughter – got married and went away to live in the trans-Yamuna area, Sheila and her husband had just each other. Now Sheila had herself and only herself to rely on. And she was comforted by the routine of nursing her husband. She was a natural caregiver. She would have become despondent had her husband not needed her at every moment. Often, she awoke at night to find him crying and his bedclothes messed. She never complained as she heaved the sheets from under him, straightening the rubber mackintosh lining the bed to prevent bedsores. And then helping him over the shame of wetting his bed. Last year when their daughter persuaded her to use adult diapers for her father at night, the transition into the second childhood was complete. So much so, that he often called out, 'Ma ...' and it was Sheila who came running to soothe his forehead with eau-de-cologned towels. And then later, as dementia took hold of his mind, he started mistaking her for his mother, and after trying to correct him a few times she let it be. Perhaps the memories of his long-dead mother gave him more comfort than the tangible reality of his omnipresent wife. So she called him 'puttar' and changed his diapers.

But sometimes she got so tired. It was exhausting work – never-ending and thankless. She didn't like to complain, but she was not so young herself. So Annu had started coming over on Wednesday and Saturday afternoons so that her mother could go out and have a little time to herself. Annu was good to her father, trying to do her best by him, but he gave his daughter a hard time fretting all the while that his wife was away.

At first, Sheila spent her free afternoons pottering about the sprawling house or getting the rambling garden back into shape. Between the two, Narenderji had been the one with the green fingers, inordinately proud of his chrysanthemums and rose bushes. After his stroke, the part-time mali became full-time but he would really just sweep and mow and occasionally weed the grounds. And she was in no position to supervise his work. In fact, both she and her husband had always prided themselves on the fact that they'd rather do their own work than supervise someone else to do it. Often their relatives would argue with them and try and persuade them to hire full-time servants, but when they did try it a few times, they found they would spend as much time 'supervising' the staff and still have a house that was not as spick and span as they would like and were used to.

So now, after Annu made her take some time off, Sheila decided to try and bring back some colour into the garden. And her life. But she would be drawn back into the house as she heard her husband's slurry voice call for her over and over. Eventually her daughter forced her to take her car and get out of the house. So now, every Wednesday it was rummy afternoon and every Saturday she went for her Ram Sharnam gathering. Things were not perfect but they were all right. And it seemed better than the lives her friends led, somehow.

'Look at Tosh,' she thought, glancing over to Tosh who had slipped a finger delicately into her mouth to dislodge a bit of food from her eternally loose dentures. Her upper lip was a little red and raw from recent threading that had become an urgent necessity, for a wiry mustache had started to sprout. Tosh had grandchildren, four of them; but they had all been born abroad and were settled in far away Australia – where her son lived – and America – where her daughter had migrated. Her Australian bahu was sweet, but of course didn't understand the ways of her Indian mother-in-law. And the Australian grandson fretted and whined his way through his Indian stay.

It was no better with her daughter who'd got married to an Indian, but one who'd been in America for such a long time that he didn't really count as one. He was more American than Indian in his ways, his thoughts and emotions. Both her daughter and her son-in-law were professors, but in different, if equally prestigious, universities. And these universities weren't even in the same town. They were about six hours apart. It was all very well in the beginning, but once the babies came (and when did they get the time to make those babies: three of them, she wondered!) it was just so pointless. Their very existence seemed to be pointless, at least from the point of view of Tosh and her friends. I mean look at their lives, the father lived far away, visiting on weekends. The mother got up in the morning and packed her babies off to daycare and school. She left the house without breakfast and without even making the beds! She 'caught' coffee and a donut on the way to work, as they say there, as though it was a virus or a cold. She was at work till six in the evening. In the meantime, the children went to school and from there they found their way to daycare or swimming lessons or dancing lessons or some such thing. Then she picked up the kids from wherever they happened to be that day of the week. She carted them back home; often enough they called in for dinner, for where was the time and energy left for a home-cooked meal? And that was it. They slept – on unmade beds. What kind of life was that? The children didn't know their parents. The parents didn't see their children grow up.

Once when the topic came up for the nth time, Tosh's daughter snapped back at her, 'Oh ho, ma, how can I give up my career for my children?' And Tosh left the room, eyes burning from unshed tears, feeling she had failed as a parent. 'No, no, no,' her heart protested, 'how can you give up your *children* for your *career*?' But she hadn't said anything, for what was the point? Children these days thought so differently. Her daughter had forgotten her Indian ethos and become more American than the Americans themselves, probably.

So she tried to make it up to her grandchildren. She visited them in the States for long spells. She tried to be there when they got home, greeting them with a fresh smile to garnish the freshly baked cookies or namak paras she'd been busy with all afternoon. She would persuade her daughter and son-in-law to let them skip some of their after-school classes so she could read to them from the Amar Chitra Katha comics and the children's Ramayan and Mahabharat she brought along. 'They should know something about Indian values and culture,' she said. So they'd sit with their Nani (although they wondered about this as their friends called their Nani 'Nanna' and they couldn't understand why it was different with Indians).

But when she stepped back to observe the situation dispassionately, she realized the children were quite happy with their lot. They *liked* to be left alone. And then she realized with some horror that they really didn't want her there with them all the time, they felt stifled by so much adult attention and they resented giving up their endless extra, after-school activities in order to spend time with their grandmother. And the little one had once innocently asked why they stopped calling in for pizzas when Nani was around. Of course, she thought, they prefer what they've grown up eating, why should they like home-made samosas now?

So she hardly got to know them and she felt the parents hardly knew each other .... 'They're just strangers who share a bed, really.' She had shared these thoughts with Sheila once when she'd gone over to be with her at the time when Sheila's husband was in hospital. There, in the strangely sanitized intimacy of the hospital room, Tosh shared with her these terrible secrets, but made Sheila promise not to tell the others. She had never broken the promise and these shared secrets brought the two friends closer.

'Hai hai, Sheila, tu kee karni hai? Khedna hai te khed, nahin te go home and do your daydreaming.' Tosh broke in into Sheila's reverie.

'Sorry, sorry, I was just thinking about you, Tosh.'

'About me? What were you thinking – what nice cakes I bake???'

'No, well, y-yes, that and the fact that your grandchildren don't know what they're missing, not having you around them, baking for them, looking after them.'

'Arrey, I know, and that silly daughter of mine and the even sillier son-in-law keep asking and asking me to come, but you know how it was when I went last summer ....'

'It can't have been all that bad?'

'What not that bad? What's the fun if everybody is out all day long, busy with their this-class and that-class and I'm just waiting and waiting – I mean, what's the point? Frankly, they prefer their burgers-shergers and hot dogs-vot dogs to the stuff I bake anyway and they want to go to all those hundred classes as though they haven't been in school all day long as it is. Pehle toh it was fun, there was so much shopping and all to do, the malls used to just dazzle me. But now: look, you can get everything you want right here, every imported item is available. And you are in the comfort of your home. You have your servants ....'

'I swear, who wants to manjho bartans and sweep the floors there when we've never done it in all our lives, na?'

'And you have your friends, you have us.'

'Yes, I have you. And I don't want to give it all up.'

'But, your grandchildren ...?'

Kunti Chadda was quick to bite into the conversation. This was a topic on which she had a lot to say. 'Arrey, grandchildren-shandchildren, what's the big deal? I tell you, I think Tosh-behenji has made a very wise decision to stay where she is the master of her own home. Look at me, my sons sold our home with the promise that I would live with them after Pritamji died. I live with them, but now, in the last years of my life, what do I get? I was a maharani in my own home, I tell you, a maharani. Pritamji never let me lift a finger to do any work. Pampered me royally, he did. And now? Now I'm just a glorified ayah to these brats of my brats!' Kunti's voice had risen to a high-pitched treble, cruelly mimicking her daughter-in-law, 'All the time it's Mataji, we have to go out for a very important dinner party, please can you feed the children their khana and then make sure Dhruvi does his homework? And give Manasi her homeopathic medicine and do this and do that, phalana-dhamkana ... it never ends. Bah! Grandchildren and this joint-family business are overrated. It's just a smart way of getting free labour from us elders.' Kunti Chadda was unstoppable once she got started on her woes.

Tosh was amused but disapproving, but it was Satya who spoke up in her 'poor-me' voice.

'Kya Kunti, don't speak like that about your own flesh and blood.'

'Flesh and blood? Yes, flesh and blood is right, they'll eat my flesh and drink my blood if I don't watch out!' she was on a roll now and oblivious to the gasps of shock and disapproval from her friends.

'Dekh, you don't know how blessed you are. The sound of laughter and voices ...,' Satya was not ready to relinquish the mike as yet. She had convinced herself years and years ago that her story was the sorriest lot of all. And she determinedly stuck to her unenviable position at the top of the 'Poor-Me ladder' as though it were a hard-won prize.

'The sound of fighting and bickering, more like ....'

'Okay, okay, the sound of bickering and fighting: at least these are the sounds of people you love, people who love you, care for you, look after your needs.'

'Kya look after my needs? Rubbish! There's no looking after my needs. Dare I say that I want to watch one of my serials on TV – bas, it is as if I have asked for the moon.' Once again she used her bitchy high-pitched imitation. 'Mataji, please, there's a cricket match, you can watch your serials any time. Please Mataji, let the children watch their cartoons just now.'

'But you got your own TV, didn't you?'

'Yes of course, I took your advice and got it, but do you think it helped?'

'Didn't it?'

'No, not at all. Now when I want to watch TV, it is usually "too loud". Bhai, can I help it if I can't hear so well? It's "Mataji, your TV is loud, Dhruv has exams", or "I have a headache", or ... or ... if I am watching something, it's "Mataji, please could you feed Manasi, she is fussing, and we have to go out". Or, "please could the children watch TV in your room, we have very important guests". Oh, something or the other is always up. Something more important than me enjoying the last days of my life. I tell you, it wasn't always like this.'

'Oh ho, really Kunti, why do you always go on about your last days? A good hatti-katti like you has a lifetime of last days left.' Satya pinched Kunti's flappy upper arms in an almost friendly way. She herself had skin stretched so tight over her bones it was as if there was nothing in between. Kunti bristled at this comment on her bulges, but held her own.

The last hand was played out with all the women in good spirits. No one paid too much attention to Satya who was a bit miffed that the talk had not settled on her loneliness. She frowned at Kunti, seeing her in a deeper shade of purple than ever before. A drama-queen purple.

Kunti's bad mood had lifted a bit as she won the hand with many points. They 'settled' their winnings and losses instantly, doling out the money. The stakes they played for were low so no one would feel uncomfortable, but they were careful to settle it instantly so money would never be an issue between them. That was one of the reasons their friendship had lasted all these years.

The four women were friends since boarding school, in the prestigious St Bede's Convent in Simla where girls were brought up to be proper young women with good values: readied for marriage that should never be too far in the horizon. They were a feisty lot then, and had remained a feisty set of friends even now, 'in their last days', as Kunti so often liked to say. They had so much in common then, from waxing their legs to painting their fingernails, from boys to men. And husbands. Then children. Once they had finished school and gone off to different colleges, they had tried to meet once a month, or at least once or twice a year.

On one such monthly meeting Tosh told them that Simmi – a classmate from school – had landed up in hospital. They went to see her in the hospital instead of going out for their lunch and they were shocked to see the bruises and fractures she'd sustained in a violent beating by her husband. Simmi was one of the first in the group to get married. They'd all been to her wedding. They'd been the sakhis who brought the bride out and giggled when she hit them on their heads with her silvery kaleeras so that they would get married soon. The next time they met up in their group, they had giggled and gurgled over the thrill of imagining her wedding night.

Now seeing her in hospital, battered and defeated, they held her wounded hand as she sobbed and asked them to let her die. 'I can't go back to him, I won't go back.'

They could do nothing for Simmi right then, except wipe her tears. Simmi's family was very conservative and the girls did not have the courage to discuss this with any of them, although their hearts broke when they heard that a week later Simmi was carted off to her husband's house unceremoniously. But when the four friends met up the next time, they took a pledge never to accept being slapped or hit. They pricked their fingers as Kunti insisted. They pressed drops of blood into each other's wounds and became 'blood sisters'. And they swore that they would stand up for each other and never let violence enter their homes. The first time Sheila's husband slapped her, she left the house. She went straight to Tosh's army-bungalow and cried and cried and cried, until Tosh was crying with her too. And then, gathering courage far beyond what they thought they had, they went back to Sheila's house and confronted her husband. He was so startled he didn't say anything as Tosh, in a sweet, gentle way told him that they would go to the police if he laid another hand on Sheila. They hadn't told the other two about it, though. It was too shameful a secret.

Now, years and deaths later, these rummy afternoons were the mainstay for each of them, each escaping her own particular circumstance, her own particular problems. Each probably thought that the other's problems were not as great as her own. But that didn't stop them from being sympathetic to each other. They depended on each other and on these afternoons to renew their oft-flagging spirits. It lifted one in the process of her lifting the other. They met in each one's house, by turns. The food was kept simple: tea, biscuits and one savoury something. This was essentially done out of consideration for Satya, whose purse was not as deep as the others', fed only by her retired teacher's pension; and no one wanted to cause her any discomfort. Much of this had never been stated, but was understood by all.

These afternoons were never missed, by any of them, if they could help it.

2

The next Wednesday, Kunti Chadda arrived at the card-game in a huge fret. She was seething. Her face was red, her blood pressure high and still rising. She stormed in.

'Hai, give me water, please someone. Give me a cold-cold glass of water.' As she flung herself down onto the waiting soft sofa – ever the drama-queen – the other three rushed to comfort her. Tosh, whose house they were meeting in that day, rushed to the kitchen calling the servant to get a glass of thanda. Satya grabbed a cushion from another chair and plumped it before slipping it behind Kunti's head so that she could lean back onto it. Sheila went to the seething Kunti calmly, sat on the arm of the chair and fished a hanky out of her bag. She patted the gently perfumed, gently embroidered kerchief onto her friend's flushed brow and soothed her with clucking sounds. They gathered around, waiting for her frayed nerves to soothe, her temper to subside. It eventually did. And the story came out along with tears earlier held in check, streaming all together out of her eyes, her mouth and nose.

'Bas, I've had it: I'm really, really fed up.' They didn't interrupt, although they were dying to ask, 'Par hua kya?'

'Dekho, selfishness ki bhi hadd hoti hai. I never brought my son up to be so, so selfish. I tell you, he is completely under the influence of that witch of a daughter-in-law of mine.' She ignored the gasp of disapproval from Satya. The flow could not be stemmed now, and well they knew it, so they held their silence and let her continue, 'I tell you, I've never seen such a badly brought-up girl. Who would have thought ... a good family, chalo, even if they were not of the same background, not as well to do as us, but I thought these Madrasi girls would be better. But no, today's younger generation is just the same, be it from Madras or Punjab. And, and, the thinner they are, the meaner they are: their generosity disappearing along with their hips and tits!' Another gasp – this time from all the others – went unheeded, although, of course Kunti had heard it and marked it off in triumph. She had recently developed a great fondness for cursing and using 'dirty' words. At first she would physically shut her ears whenever her son cursed in anger, or when their friends came over and used lots of gaalies: mazzak mazzak mein. Now Kunti often pressed her ear to the door and gleefully mugged up new curses and then stood in front of her bathroom mirror trying out the new words and planning to use it at the first opportunity that presented itself.

'They think that what they do is too important and you are bas, nothing.'

She spat out the last word, as if it were too dirty to stay in her mouth any longer.

There had been a showdown with her son and daughter-in-law. They wanted to go away for the weekend. They said they had had a very stressful time at work and needed to get away. 'Stress, hah, what stress, I ask you? Both of them sitting in air-conditioned offices the whole day long. Just look at my daughter-in-law Meera – Miss Big Star-Shar, having other people put makeup, getting her ready for the camera, just being a big star on TV. What stress does she have, I ask you? She just sits there fluttering her eyelashes at the male newsreader next to her, reading news that someone else hunts down, reading from a script that someone else has written. Stress? Bah!! They have no idea the kind of stress Pritamji had to go through. Door to door, I tell you; he went door to door selling. And me, bringing up my children single-handedly. No maids, at that time, no convenient mother-in-law to be unpaid slave. Stress, bah!' she spat again.

'So why not let them go on their holiday, Kunti, they're young, na? How does it affect your life?' asked Tosh.

'How does it not? I ask you – am I not an old lady? Am I not suffering from high blood pressure and sugar? Do I need some care or not?'

'But you won't be alone, Kunti, there are the servants – there is the ayah.'

'Ayah, hah, now you're sounding just like that witch my son has married.'

'Hai, hai, Kunti, don't talk like that about your flesh and blood.'

'Flesh and blood? Again? Again you're saying flesh-and-blood? I tell you, they'll eat me up raw and not even maaro a dikar after! Hah! They would eat my flesh and … and put my blood into chilled glasses with salt put on the rims and say cheers and drink it up, if they could!' Again she ignored the gasps. 'They also said, "there are the servants, there is the ayah".' She mimicked them horribly, cruelly.

'Hain, so there is na?'

'Did I bring up my children to leave me with an ayah? Would Pritamji ever, ever leave me with an ayah if I were not well? If Pritamji had known it was going to end like this, he would never have died before me.' She looked up in accusation, as though he had purposely died before her, just to trouble her. 'He would have taken me with him. I wish he had.' A little sob seemed to remind her of her rage. She held onto it, bursting out again, 'I told them, I told them in no uncertain terms that when they were children and they needed me, when they were sick, I never left them with an ayah. No, never, not even once! I gave up everything, everything so that I could look after my son. I was beautiful – you remember how beautiful I was? Then when times were hard, I gave up my pedicures and manicures, I gave up buying clothes like I used to. You remember how I used to buy clothes? And shoes, you remember my passion for shoes?' She looked up and smiled and found them all smiling back. With a start she realized that she had cooled off; she shook herself, sat up straight and fought to keep her anger on the boil. 'I used to soothe his fever, his hurts with these two hands. I never, ever left him with an ayah ….' She held her arms out for all to see the hands that had held her babies, the hands that had been there. *Her* hands, not the ayah's. Never the ayah's. She collapsed in fresh tears, moaning, 'I'm not well, I'm really, really not well, I tell you. Suppose something happens to me?'

'Hush, hush ….'

Water and eau-de-cologned hankies and most of all, sympathetic ears and pats eventually calmed Kunti down. But no amount of persuasion could change her mind about her son and daughter-in-law. The 'suppose something happens to me?' hung like a sword above all their heads. It was something they all dreaded, even though they wouldn't say it out loud to each other, not most of the time, anyway.

Satya, especially, had a terrible fear of the 'suppose something ...' ever since she once choked on a fish bone that got so stuck in her windpipe that she panicked and almost blacked out before she could get out of her flat and bang on the neighbour, Gopalji's door. He had helped her, calmed her down. He even called the doctor home to ensure that she was well, insisting on paying the doctor himself. But, since then, she always worried about the terrible 'something' happening to her and being unable to get help in time.

So, even as Kunti calmed down, each turned quiet. Each knew, too, that even if Kunti was being unreasonable, there was something to what she said. Each of them, in their own way, was not leading the life they would have chosen to. Each was making the compromises they were, as young girls, told were virtues. Compromise was the secret to a woman's happiness, but it hadn't brought them that much-promised happiness. Not so far, not in the foreseeable future. And of course, they didn't have very long futures ahead of them.

Their game that afternoon was somewhat subdued, although Tosh tried to inject some laughter by telling a dirty joke. She wore shell pink that afternoon, with perfectly matched opalescent nail-polish and pink pearls. Satya liked that, because it was exactly the colour she had assigned to Tosh – a mauvy pinky hue with a mild shimmer. Elegant, never garish. She leaned forward, as much to take in Tosh's summery, lemony perfume as to hear her, as Tosh said.

'Arrey, I must tell you, my daughter sent me a hilarious joke on my email.'

'Hai, Tosh, I'm so jealous, tu kinni syani hai. My grandchildren have been trying to teach me how to work the computer, but I swear, I'm so frightened, I feel as if it is a huge animal on the table that will attack me if I touch it!'

'Even I was like that, but it is really, really easy. You should just keep trying it, na.'

'Oh ho, tell your joke now.'

'I hope it's a dirty one?'

'Ooof ho, kaisi batein karti ho?'

'Actually, it is slightly dirty.'

'Good, good, toh sunao,'

'Oh, you women ...'

'Shhh ...'

'So, there was this little girl who wanted to take her dog out for a walk, but her mother wouldn't let her, because the dog was in heat.'

'Then it wasn't a dog, but a bitch, na!'

'Hai, hai, kitni gandi hai tu, Kunti.'

'Such a dirty word – bi ... oof, I can't even say it.'

'Gandi, kya? A female dog is a bitch only, na? The male dog won't be in heat – he's a man, no?'

'Except, you know, my cousin's brother-in-law has to wear sanitary pads, he has bleeding!'

'Oof, he must have piles, not periods, Satya!'

'Chee, I hate that word,' grumbled Satya, putting her hands to her ears.

'Accha, you want to hear the joke or discuss periods?'

'Chee ....'

'Hain, hain, sorry, tell, tell.'

'So the girl goes on whining.'

'Sounds like my Manasi, won't take "no" for an answer.'

'Shhhh ....'

'Finally, she goes to her father who is working on his car in the garage.'

'Then this must be a foreign joke.'

'Arrey, why?'

'Because only foreigners put their cars in their garages. If we have a garage we put it to better use; like servants' quarters or keeping our trunks and all.'

'You're right!'

'Oh ho, you want to hear the joke or not?'

'Sorry, sorry, bas, ab sub chup ho jao.'

'So the little girl goes to her father and says that she wants to take the dog out for a walk but mama won't let her. Now the father knows that the dog is in heat.'

'Then this really is a foreign joke, here no father would know such a detail.'

'Oh ho, chup bhi kar na Sheila. Chalo, Tosh, aage batao.'

'So the father takes a piece of cloth, soaks it in petrol and then wipes down the bi-bi-oof, bhai, the dog's back legs to wipe out the smell so that other dogs can't smell she's in heat. Then he tells his daughter that he has filled petrol into the dog so she can take her once around the block. Yes, Satya, now we know that it's a foreign joke, we don't have blocks, na? Anyway, he tells her that she must just take one round and then come back immediately. Off the girl goes, and sure enough, after a little while, she comes back, but without the dog. Alarmed, the father asks what happened and the little girl replies, "Papa, I was taking her, but half way round the block, she ran out of gas, now another dog is pushing her home!"'

The laughter was accompanied by lots of 'chee' and 'hai hai'. It lightened the mood a little, which was a relief, for, according to them, a serious, woeful afternoon with each other, without laughter, was a wasted afternoon.

But as they were leaving, Sheila brought up the topic again, 'Kunti, dekh, I think it will be wiser and nicer to let your daughter-in-law and son go on the holiday they've planned, doesn't matter, na? You and Pritamji used to go off on holidays, why not let them go?'

'But what if ....'

'If something happens, then we're all here na? And why think of the worst? Nothing is going to happen; you are in good health, why should you fall ill?'

'What good health? I'm not in good health, how can you say this? My sugar, my blood pressure, the pain in my knees!'

'Hain, but working yourself up like this is only going to make your BP go up, na? What's the use?' Tosh continued, 'Tell me, whenever you and Pritamji went for a holiday, did you always take your mother-in-law?'

'No, of course not,' Kunti scoffed, 'but I tell you, she was a real churail, chewing afeem and cursing, shouting. But I'm not like that, na? I'm a normal, fun person to have around. I am fun. Aren't I? Aren't I?'

'Yes, yes!' they all pitched in hurriedly in the face of her accusing gaze.

'Yes, Kunti,' Sheila said, patting her tense, tight shoulders, 'you are a fun person, but young people need their family outings. You know that. And, and if you force them to call off their holiday, you'll just be guilty and feel awful and they will be upset and sulking, koi faida hoga kya?'

Kunti was quiet; she knew in her heart of hearts that Sheila was right, but still …

'I just wish they'd consider taking me with them …'

And that was the crux of the matter, wasn't it: there was this need, no, this hunger to feel included, to be an inseparable part of a whole. She only really felt needed – *really* needed – here, at the rummy gatherings where the game could not, or would not happen without all of them present. She felt sick and unhappy to be left out, unwanted. To be dispensable.

3

The daughter-in-law persuaded her husband that there was really nothing wrong with his mother. 'She's just making a fuss for nothing, she's perfectly well, and you know it.'

Of course he did. He knew that his mother was just being difficult and there was nothing extraordinarily wrong with her. But he did feel guilty and although he didn't want to admit it to himself, the truth was it was a decision he didn't want to be guilty of taking. Just in case something – oh, anything – went wrong, his wife would take the blame. She'd have to; after all, it was her decision.

He just went along with it, that's all. He was a bit like that. Satya had diagnosed him a long time ago as a grey – neither here nor there. Neither white nor black. Just grey. His wife, of course, was Satya's orange. Bright, glittery. Very beautiful. A bit too loud to be a wife and a mother. Certainly too strong a shade to be a good bahu!

So they went, under a cloud of grumbles, complaints and scowls. They left, waving cheerful goodbyes, promising to get a good cardigan and moisturizer and Bengay for her aching knees.

Kunti didn't want another cardigan. She had one in every colour and she was happy enough with the moisturizers she could go down to the colony shops and buy for herself. Now you could buy every brand and everything almost anywhere. What was the use of them bringing things? She, after all, needed to have something to do, even if it was just going to the shops and buying it herself. She needed Bengay, of course, but, they didn't need to go away to get it ... she had heard that even her favourite brand of balm was now available in some chemist shops, although she'd never actually managed to get it herself.

She pottered about the empty house, trying – desperately trying, honestly – not to mind too much. Now that they were gone, she tried to make some sense of the advice her friends had given: 'let them go'. She had let them go. Now she tried not to mind their going, their leaving her, too much. But the house was empty. Very, very empty. And, despite herself, she felt her tears welling up. Although she tried hard not to, she sat on the sofa that she had chosen for her son's wedding and let the sobs roll out of her tight, tight throat. There were more tears in her than she had bargained for. She cried for a long, long time. Even when the phone started to ring, she couldn't stem the flow of her tears and could not bring herself to answer it. Let one of the maids do it, she thought. Probably a call for them anyway. Nowadays, the maids got more phone calls than she did.

But it was for Kunti. Her son calling from the airport. It took her a while to be able to get more than just a hello out of her tear-pinched throat. She was happy for a few moments, thinking he had after all cared, hoping, futilely – she knew – they had changed their minds. But her hope changed to ashes when she heard his furtive, whispery voice. He was hiding the fact he was calling his own mother. Hiding the fact from his own family. Shame, she thought, shame!

'Why are you whispering?' She demanded, aggressively, 'You don't want your darling wife to know you are phoning your witch of a mother?'

'Ma, please, please, don't make this harder.'

'Harder? Harder? Harder for who – for you? How is this hard for you, I ask you? It's hard for me, but for you – how can you accuse me of making it harder? It is you who make things hard. You, who do not even have the guts to tell your wife you want to make a phone call to your own mother? Just one bloody phone call!'

'What?' His voice was snappy now, 'What the hell are you talking about?'

'Don't you dare, don't you dare take out these gaalies in front of me! Don't think I can't give gaalies back. Just because, just because I'm a decent, god-fearing woman and don't keep saying Fuck this Fuck that like you, doesn't mean ... don't think I can't. I can. Fuck! Fuck! Fuck! See? See?'

Before she could stop herself, she slammed the receiver down and her hands flew off the phone as if they'd been burned. She was shaking with anger, was in a raging inferno of a fury. How dare he, how dare he?

And then it happened. The nausea and dizziness hit her like a double slap across the face, coming at her from both directions. She felt the world go a little darker; her head became light and heavy at the same time. She leaned forward, immediately wanting to call her son and tell him he needed to come home at once. But the nausea gagged her and she blacked right out. Like a power cut, her lights went out.

The ayah came in only a few minutes later and her first reaction was to start screaming. She screamed and screamed and finally it had the desired effect as the girl who did the cooking and the watchman came rushing in response to her shouts. Together they splashed water onto Mataji's face and lifted her up just as she started to revive. They laid her onto the sofa that stood in front of the TV; the phone was close by. Jemima, the cook, who was by far the coolest of the lot, rushed to her quarter and fished out the diary in which she had her phone numbers. She flipped to the page where she had sahib's number as she was making her way to her very own mobile. She dialed and waited and waited. It was taking too long. She tried again and this time got a voice almost immediately.

'The number you have dialed has been switched off. Please try again later,' said a voice that had more cheer in it than Jemima felt just now. 'No, no, wait,' she shouted, before she realized she was talking to a pre-recorded voice. She flipped to memsahib's number, but got the same response. Their phones were switched off. They were obviously on their flight.

Jemima had flown with them to a lovely cottage in Goa once, where the whole family, except Mataji of course, went for a holiday. Well, it was a holiday for everyone else, but not for her. She'd cooked morning, noon and late into the night. Anyway, that's how she knew mobile phones had to be switched off in the plane. What now?

Mataji had revived a little. She was sitting up and Shanti had gone to make nimbu pani for her. 'Mataji, what happened?' Jemima asked, looking worriedly into the rather flushed face before her. But after telling the whole story, Mataji insisted the doctor not be bothered. No amount of persuasion would change her mind.

Finally Jemima settled the old lady onto the sofa itself, since she did not feel steady enough to make it to the bedroom. As Jemima went to her bedroom to get Mataji's glass for soaking her teeth, her moisturizer and some other things she would need in the next few hours, she spotted

Mataji's diary lying next to her phone on the bedside table. This gave her an idea. She decided she would make some calls. There was no need to ask for permission. She was in charge and she felt it was necessary; after all, suppose something were to happen during the night? How could she take responsibility like this?

'Hello, Sheila bhabiji?'

'Yes …?'

'Bhabiji, mein Jemima, you know, the cook, from Kunti Mataji's house.'

Immediately the voice at the other end, which had been soft and tentative grew stronger, more concerned, 'Hain hain, Jemima beta, kya hua, sab theek thak toh hai na. Everything ok?'

Jemima couldn't help a little flush of pleasure at the 'beta'. Truly, Sheila bhabiji was a gem of a lady; she treated Jemima like her own child. So generous, Sheila bhabi even gave her a shawl this last Diwali, although she didn't even work for her.

'Jemima, beta, kaise phone kiya?'

Eventually, it was Tosh Bhatia who came to be with Kunti and she brought her BP and blood sugar testing machines with her. The blood sugar and pressure were both high. Not alarmingly so, but high enough for Tosh to order a dinner of saltless khichdi and a handful of jamuns, that were luckily in the fridge, for her friend. For herself, she had brought her usual dinner of clear veg soup and multi-grain bread. She ate healthily, always trying to lose weight, reading every diet column and article and trying each one. It didn't really help; she was still unable to wear the Western clothes she'd bought for herself from abroad. She fitted into them, but was honest enough to admit they didn't look too good. She looked lumpy and ungainly.

She got the maids to lay a bed for her in the guest room and put a fresh towel in the bathroom. She was pleased at how well trained these girls were. A new soap, a new toothbrush, a hotel shampoo and toothbrush, complete with a single use toothpaste tube. All laid out for her. She felt suddenly happy, then immediately guilty for feeling so. Happy, because she felt relieved of her own loneliness. This was a little like a holiday. Then came the guilt because she was, after all, here to look after a sick friend, one who had fainted. She took one last look around her room for the night, pulled out her book and her nightly laxative and put these on the bedside table, ready for later.

She had managed to get Kunti to her bed with the help of the maids. She settled herself on the comfy sofa chair next to her friend and put her feet up on a low stool. Their food was brought in by the maids just as Kunti and Tosh had all the remotes they would need between them: the TV remote, the dish TV remote, CD player remote, the cordless phone, the AC remote, both their mobiles and, of course, the remote bell to call the maids if they needed either of them.

'Ah,' sighed Tosh, trying to cheer her friend up, 'this is life, isn't it Kunti?' And Kunti waited for the rush of resentment to well up inside, but was quite, quite surprised when it didn't. Instead, a warm contentment spread through her: 'Yes ...,' she whispered in a surprised whisper, 'yes, you know, you're right. This is life!' And Tosh smiled too for she realized that she was not saying this only to cheer her friend, but because she felt the same contentment.

Tosh was a creature of strict habit. Well balanced. Gentle – like the mauvy pink Satya had assigned to her, although, of course she didn't know that. But just the right amount. Not too much, not too little. Not too loud and bright, not so pale as to fade into the background. Everything in her well-ordered house went like clockwork. Everything was in its place. She never had to look for her keys, she never lost a piece of jewellery. Her maid went on Sundays for her chutti and the cook once a month. She had her massage lady come in every Tuesday and went for her 'denting painting' as the friends called it, once a month. Even the denting painting was set – manicure, pedicure, arms waxing, veg. peel and thermomask, hair dye – number 3.5 and trim – just 2 cms. Her hair never showed its grey roots. Her moustache never bristled, her eyebrows never straggled. The colour of her nails was always the same – White Wand – a lovely silvery, metallic look or Mauve Mist.

Her cupboard was a treat to her eyes every time she opened it's well-polished doors. Pale pastels, always. Puces and pinks, lilacs and lemons. The beige chiffon sari, with tiny sequins and Swarovski crystals though was a favourite. Dressy but classy. A rare splurge. Each sari hung with its own blouse and petticoat. There was a matching nara in every petticoat, not those rolls of white naras for her. Each salwar kameez hung with its own chunni. While she preferred the delicacy of the lightweight, gossamer fabrics like crepe and chiffon, she had also got a few cotton suits and duppattas from Fabindia. Her sister said a more ethnic look suited her. She never bought any of these herself. Her sister bought these for her for every birthday. But for herself, she preferred the clothes her husband had liked her to wear. Clothes that made her look fair and elegant and proper, in the 'propah' army circles to which they had belonged.

She had loved her husband dearly. They'd been such a good match. Both ordered, controlled, calm and efficient. They rarely raised their voices at each other or at the servants, orderlies and batmen who catered to their every need. Both were rather frugal, although not exactly stingy. Saving up for their children's education, saving up so that when the time came, they could send them abroad for further studies, even at a time when it wasn't so common. But they had lived well within their means, no one ever really guessing they were saving so much. Both of them were innately elegant and even clothes verging on faded were worn with pride. She could mix her blouses and saris and jewellery with such élan it would look like she was wearing a new outfit and some of the other women would comment, with curling lips, how much she spent on her clothes. But when, as the children grew up, the elder one went to Australia for graduation and the younger one to a fairly expensive private boarding school, people could not hide their surprise. A few snide comments that were made about how they must have either inherited some money, or 'had made some money somewhere' didn't bother them. They smiled as they waved their children off into the world. And soon enough, they were rewarded when both the siblings earned scholarships, topping their classes. And then, even after her husband passed away, she was able to help fund the younger one's post-graduation at a prestigious university in the US. Soon after, they settled down to well-paid jobs and later acquired well-placed spouses.

Now she looked around, coming back to the present as she realized with surprise she was really quite pleased to have been shaken out of her set evening routine of early dinner and reading the *Hanuman Chalisa* before turning in for the night. She always swore she hated watching TV at night for it disturbed her pastel coloured dreams. But now, here was Kunti, flipping channels furiously and muttering they were not, just not going to see the news channels or anything serious or tragic.

Finally they stopped at the Fashion TV channel, but after a giggly ten minutes got quite bored with skinny models so slight that their braless breasts didn't even jiggle. 'Hai, hai, faida kya hua inka? What would their men have to hold onto, I say?' laughed Kunti.

'Shh, oof, how you talk, Kunti,' said Tosh trying to sound disapproving, but laughing instead. How do these girls nowadays have children? Where do they keep the baby? They have no hips, no stomachs, nothing! They giggled and openly, loudly, demanded from the TV screen it show some men instead. But, they were not in luck that night!

'Doesn't matter, Kunti, you're not even well, maybe we should just turn in for the night. Bhai, I'm used to a very early night and you should sleep too, hain na?'

'Yes, I suppose you're right,' said Kunti, not feeling sleepy and not feeling unwell at all. 'You know ...,' she began, but then kept quiet for a bit, wondering how to say it, how to give words to the thought that had just crossed her mind.

'You know ... you all were right. It's true, I am fine, there's nothing really wrong with me. I feel like such a fool.'

'Why? Why should you feel like a fool, Kunti? Of course not.'

'No, you were right and I refused to listen. Of course I'm well. I don't know why I got into such a rage about it and made myself ill; I should have let them go happily, not made such a fuss about things, no?'

'Arrey, koi baat nahin ...'

'No, I mean, I feel guilty now, I'm sure I've spoilt their holiday ...'

'Oh ho, so when they call, just tell them to go have a good time, that you're all right, na? Then they'll all be happy.'

'Yes, yes, you're right, I'll do just that, arrey, why don't I listen to you, you're so much more sensible.'

'That's true! But good na, now you're listening – and they say you can't teach an old dog new tricks!'

'Not dog, remember – bitch!'

'Oof, Kunti, you're getting from bad to worse!'

'Oh, you've no idea how much worse I've been.'

'Why, what did you do now?'

'Hai, I can't tell you, I'm so ashamed.'

Tosh waited, knowing the other was dying to spill the beans and unburden herself.

'Hai, Tosh, I feel so silly, you can't imagine the gandi gandi gaalies I gave my son. F word and all!'

'Haw! Chalo, koi nahin, when he calls, just tell him sorry, aur kya?'

'I – I'm really sorry, Tosh, I truly am sorry.'

'Now what?'

'Well, I have inconvenienced you like this, no. Making you come over like this, suddenly. Giving you a fright.'

Tosh was quiet for a moment, then she took her friend's hand in her own and confessed she was happy, too happy to have had a reason to snap out of her routine, to have her tight little boat rocked a little. 'It will do me some good, I think. I have to confess, Kunti, I've never admitted this, not even to myself, but it sometimes worries me how set I've become in my ways. So much so I sometimes really worry how I'll manage if something really goes wrong and I have to do things out of routine, you know? And, and – oh I hate to say it, but its true. You know, when my grandchildren come and leave the remote on a chair, or their packet of chips and glasses all over and my house turns upside down – even a bit ... well, I can't stand it. Sometimes I have to go to the bathroom and wash my face to calm myself down. Sometimes, well, once, at least once ... I even wished they'd – oh I'm so ashamed to say it – I even wished they would go. And leave everything – my home, my remotes, my fridge – oh everything to me ...,' she sighed, shook her head and rubbed her eyes, 'I'm so ashamed, but, but I did, I did wish they, my own family, my flesh and blood would just – just – go.'

The two friends were silent, embarrassed by the admission. Embarrassed also by the fact both of them had wished the same thing: to be left alone to have a life, run a home, just as they wanted.

'So have I,' Kunti finally admitted, 'I love my grandchildren. To tell you the truth, I'm so very proud of my daughter-in-law, although she can be a bit harsh sometimes. I know she is under a lot of stress. I can't imagine what it is to be a working wife, a working mother. I get irritated, of course, that she just presumes I'll do things she should be doing but cannot because she has to go to work at all odd hours. But still, every time someone tells me she is so beautiful or they liked a programme of hers on TV I swell up with pride. We go to a wedding or something, and people are pointing at her, staring; I do feel so proud. I feel proud to be with her, to call her my own. I like to stand next to her, bask in her fame, you know? And yet, and yet ... Oh Tosh, I'm so glad to hear you say this. I too have wished the same. And how guilty I felt for feeling like this,' she finished in a gush of emotion.

'And how very silly of you. Now that you have the house to yourself, when you can watch your TV at full blast without any tok-taak, you are wasting the golden opportunity by lying around like an invalid feeling resentful!'

'Oh my goodness, I never thought of it like that! I tell you, how silly we are, no?'

'Yes, yes, we are ....' Tosh was quiet for a moment and then broke out into a grin. A real, child-like grin. 'Tell you what, let's not just go to sleep early like we always do. Let's do something completely different from our usual routine. What can we do, Kunti?'

'Ooh, good idea, I know, let's watch a movie. Dekh, the children have loads of movies in that cupboard, let's choose one and watch it late into the night – what do you say?'

So it was decided. Tosh wouldn't let Kunti get up out of bed 'just in case.' Instead, she went and brought a few DVDs from the living room. She also brought some chips and some Coke for them to drink. They giggled at their own naughtiness. Eventually, because they were in a 'naughty child mood,' as Kunti so aptly put it, they chose to watch *Jungle Book*, enjoying the lively animated film and laughing and singing along. They knew the songs from when they'd sung along with their grandchildren. This time they enjoyed singing them just for themselves. They even stood up for the vultures' song, holding out their own wizened arms and singing to each other on top of their lungs, 'We're your friends, we're your friends till the bitter end ....'

And then they slept in late the next morning, forgetting to have their laxatives, leaving crumbs of chips on the floor and water stains on the side tables where they'd left them, carefully pushing away the coasters. Neither of them had ever had a night like this in a long time.

4

The next time the group got together, there appeared to be a special bond between the two friends who had spent that memorable night together. There was a fair amount of 'remember this' and 'how we did that'! In fact, as if on cue, as if they had practiced it, although they had not, Kunti and Tosh jumped up and burst into the vultures' song from *Jungle Book*, 'We're your friends, We're your friends ....'

Sheila was wistful, wishing she could have a night devoid of all her responsibilities. 'Oh for even just one whole night of sleep, without waiting for him to call out, his bed wet again.'

At first the others enjoyed it, taking pleasure in their friends' joy, imagining incidents as they were narrated. But after almost an hour of it, they were mildly irritated. Noticing this, Tosh tried to change the topic. But it all came out, everyone's envious outburst when Kunti said, patting Tosh's hand, 'Bas, if it wasn't for Tosh's calming presence that night, I could have landed up in hospital and spoilt it for the children. And most especially for myself.'

Satya laughed, a little bitterness edging her voice, 'Vah, Tosh, she just listens to you, na? How long I've been saying the same thing, but does she take my advice? No, no, but Tosh behenji says the very same thing and now look, look, Kunti is all smiles! And who on earth would have thought of calling me? The maid calls Sheila behenji and she, of course, turns to Toshi. Satya ko kaun yaad karta hai museebat mein? After all, I'm not to be trusted in a crisis, am I?' she laughed her high-pitched laugh, pretending it was a very funny joke, but the bitter edge gave her away.

'Don't say that, Satya,' Sheila, ever the comforter, came to the rescue as everyone looked uncomfortable. 'Please don't be like that, you know it's not true.'

'Oh ho, it was just a joke.'

Kunti explained, 'I know you were all telling me the same thing, Satya. Each and every one of you was telling me that I was being silly. But then, when I had that attack and Tosh was kind enough to come and stay with me, we had such a good time. Well, that's when I realized that you all were right. I could be having such fun, I should be enjoying my freedom, not grumbling and throwing fits ...'

'And making yourself ill.'

'And giving us all a fright!'

'Yes, but you know, if you hadn't, then I wouldn't have come over and we would not have had so much fun, no?' Tosh pointed out.

'Hain, that saying is right, "Ishwaram yat karoti, shobhanam karoti"!'

'Truly, what the Almighty does, he always does for the best – no doubt.'

'Sheila, you always have the correct saying for the correct moment.'

'By the way, how is your husband, any better?'

A quiet descended. No, Sheila's husband was not better, 'He's sinking, slowly slipping away, no matter what I do.'

'Oh Sheila, you can't do much more, my dear, eventually, it isn't in your hands no?'

'You can do what you are doing to make him comfortable and leave the rest to God.'

'Ah, I know ... and yet ... it's ... I'm trying to keep him with me, but like sand, his life is trickling through my fingers. Like sand.' She looked at her fingers, as if she could really see the life of her dear dear husband slip through them. Tosh held her hands, covering them with her own. They were quiet, each remembering their own losses. Tosh and Kunti had both lost their husbands. Tosh's husband, a proud military man, had passed away many years ago. While she was still young, her children still unsettled and unmarried. She got a lot of family support. Her brothers and brothers-in-law all gathered around her, taking care of her every need. Her husband's battalion too, was so good, so good. And yet, the aching void – missing him, missing the life she had led with him, sucked her down ever so often, even now. She never showed these dark moments to anyone. That's not what her husband would have wanted; but sometimes she sank in so deep she almost felt the need to go and join her husband. To take her own life. She didn't of course, her husband would never forgive her if she had. But oh sometimes, it was the only thing she wanted. She regretted that these friends of hers had never really known him. They had met him, of course, but only at each one's wedding, or some such occasion where there wasn't any real conversation. At that time, he was posted out of the city. She went with him as often as she could. At least until the children got into their board years. And of course, she couldn't join him when he was posted to non-family stations. She scanned the dailies avidly, sat glued to the television, her ears stuck to the bulletins on the radio, gleaning any little bit of news on the skirmishes at the borders where her husband was posted. He had seen action in one of the 1971 Indo-Pakistan wars. It was a terrible, hard time. She worried about him, staying up night after sleepless night. But she never showed it in public. She consoled and counseled the jawans' wives. They depended on her strength, although it depleted her and left her exhausted. But she never showed it. Only in the afternoons, when the servants went away to rest or late at night, after the children were in bed, she'd sneak into the kitchen, like a chor in her own home and raid the tins of namkeens, the vacuum-sealed bottles of biscuits and if all else failed, then just bread with butter or malai skimmed off the top of the children's whole milk. As her hips, stomach and chins expanded, her husband never once said anything. She hated herself for it, but the worse she felt, the more she needed to raid the fridge. The more he was away, the more she ate. Slowly, she had to buy new blouses and kameezes. But when she found even her petticoats wouldn't fit anymore, she decided, bas, enough was enough. And she gave up her sneak feasts once and for all. Her husband encouraged her by signing her up for yoga classes or walking with her if he had the time. But he wasn't around long enough to see her struggle her way back from obesity. He would have been proud, she knew, and would forgive her the slight lumpiness that remained. A few times she slipped and went back to using food to comfort her through her loss. But knowing what he would like her to do, how he would like her to be, she garnered the will power and strength to persist with her diets and exercise. She was the perfect army wife, even after her husband was gone. Strong, self-sufficient and positive.

Kunti's husband had been the centre of her universe. She had been the frail one and he was perpetually worried about her health. He was the hatta katta one. He had such good habits for himself. Running at least five miles every day, then walking instead, as the doctor advised for his knees. He walked wherever he could. Sometimes he would walk to a movie theatre or dinner or the club while she joined him in the car. He ate small, frequent meals, had his two whiskies almost every evening. Never more, sometimes less. His skin shone like it had been polished, not a sweaty shine, but a nice healthy one. A glow, really. He sported a full head of hair and began graying only when he was fifty. He never slept too late, never woke too late. If they were at an evening where dinner was served late, he would not eat at all, coming home and helping himself to some biscuits and a glass of skimmed milk instead. He was one of the paragons of good health. At breakfast he would give her vitamins and calcium tablets, urging her to be more health-conscious. But he never nagged her to exert in exercise or diet. And how he looked after her through her many niggling ailments, nursing her oh so tenderly through every cold or sprained ankle. And especially through her hysterectomy when she lost not only physical health, but confidence as well. After her operation, he even started keeping the karva chauth fasts with her, saying he would fast for her good health just as she fasted for his. One year, she had a splitting headache by the afternoon. He came home to find her feeling dizzy and nauseous with it, but he knew she would not break the fast so easily. So he feigned illness, pretending he was ready to pass out and needed a cup of tea. Then he made her drink it instead, feeding her spoonfuls, and only pretending to drink it himself.

And he spoilt her like a favourite child, taking her on the best vacations, buying her jewellery even when there was no occasion for it. They had a good marriage. The only instances of fights between them were when the children were little and he felt jealous she was spending too much time with them. She would always say that she had three children and the biggest of them was her husband!

But he went so suddenly. She wasn't even there. She was spending a few days with her sister who was having a hysterectomy and suddenly she got a call saying the maid found him dead in his bed. It was a massive heart attack. It brought her lovely life to a screeching halt. And she had resented everyone and everything since then. Especially her sister. She couldn't help it. She couldn't help the sneaking resentment that slithered through her, she couldn't help thinking that if she had been home instead, in bed with her husband, then she would have been alerted when he first got uncomfortable. She would have seen the early signs, she would have called the doctor, taken him to the hospital. Instead, she was away from him, with her sister who needed her, yes, but not as much as him. Hers had not been a life and death situation.

When she got back home, he would have – should have – been there to greet her back. Instead, she walked into the house to find it turned upside down, along with her life. The furniture moved outside, her beautiful, beautiful living room covered with white. White sheets, white-faced, white-clothed people, the wet whiteness of ice, slowly puddling onto the floor. The white sheet, the white shroud.

She leaned over him, looking into the white cotton wool stuffed into his nostrils. The white hand of her brother gripped hers as she tried to take that cotton wool out. 'But he won't be able to breathe …,' she pleaded to her brother before turning back to her husband as her tears spilled out onto his cheeks, wetting them. 'Look!' she cried, 'look, he's crying, he's crying, because he always cries if I cry!' Her brother tried to draw her to him: the brother of hers who had promised to protect her, year after year, with every rakhi she tied to his wrist. What kind of protection was this? He had not managed to keep the one thing that would keep her protected, what was the use of all those years of rakhis?

'Why didn't you save him, why didn't you save him? Why couldn't you keep him safe for me?' She sobbed, she screamed. 'You promised to protect me, how could you let this happen to me, how could you let this happen to me? You promised!'

She ran her fingers through Pritam's still-black hair. He didn't even dye it, like she had just started doing. His hair was thick, lustrous, jet black except for the few streaks of gray at his temples. He was too young to die. He was too healthy to die. She was the sickly one. She was the one supposed to go before him. How was she going to manage now? This was not how they had planned it. He was too young. Too young to be lying here, prone, unspeaking, eyes closed, nostrils stuffed with cotton wool, lying so cold, so cold on ice. She called out, 'Rani, Rani …,' the maid came at a run, hugging her, breaking, breaking into her arms, 'Rani, tum dekh nahin rahe ho? Saab ko thand lag jayegee, yeh baraf hatao, shawl lao sahib ke liye ...' But nobody moved. How could they leave him so cold? Why was Rani not running to get the shawl, why was she being so disobedient? The air was thick with moans and tears. Finally, her sister arrived. This was too much for Kunti, this was just too much ....

A chasm opened up between Kunti and her sister. She couldn't tell her, of course, but perhaps her sister knew. She knew it was not fair of her to feel this resentment, but still ... She just felt so keenly the unfairness of what had happened to her. Often she was told how lucky the was that he had gone without any illness. No hospitals, no pain ... but it didn't make it any easier. She never felt lucky after that. And time does not heal the wounds as it is supposed to. It is hard, harder, to accept, even now. And she cannot help slipping again and again into the whiteness of that dreadful day that stole the colour of her life.

Satya also thought of all she had lost. And all she had never even begun to gain. The chance to even feel that love, be a little spoilt, have something to colour the barrenness of her landscape, the desert of her womb. They may all be grieving. But at least they *had* someone to grieve over. Society was kind to widows, but it mocked spinsters cruelly. The very word – spinster – conjured up a witch spinning in a lonely tower. Spinning and spinning – cloth that would never adorn a loved one. She looked down at her own hands, arthritic and painfully thin. She twisted the diamond ring she had bought for herself on her fiftieth birthday. It was a happy secret for her until that day in the staff-room at school, when someone noticed and asked about the ring. There was so much oohing and aahing over it and so many questions about who had given it to her. She was overwhelmed and giggled and let out the truth, 'No, no, there's no one special, of course not. Not at my age, bhai, I bought this for myself!' Satya still flushed with embarrassment when she recalled the deathly silence that followed the announcement. The shock on those faces, the bitchy glances and sneaky smiles exchanged between those who flashed bigger rings presented by Men. It had taken the joy out of the purchase and after a few days she stopped wearing the ring all together. Then, when she retired, she took it out of the locker once again. As she slid it onto her ring finger, she promised herself she would not take it off for anyone or anything. It was no less precious, the diamonds no less lustrous, just because she had bought it for herself. She had to wind some knitting wool onto the band as the ring became quite loose as she lost weight, the plumpness of youth being replaced by the boniness of spinsterish age. Never mind, she loved it still.

But now all of them were losing that centre of their universe. The last amongst them, Sheila, was on the brink of widowhood herself. It was a somber thought. She had prepared for his going for so long, but now, as the time came closer, they could see the birds of sadness nesting in her eyes.

The women played on, dealing out the cards. The game cheered them up, even through the sadness and imminent loss.

5

The next rummy session was incomplete. No Sheila. At first Satya, whose house the session was at, felt irritated. She had a sneaking suspicion that Sheila did not like to come to her simple – okay, overly simple – flat. In fact, none of them did. They often made excuses like, 'Oh, why do you want to strain yourself in this heat, Satya? Let's have it at my house, let the servants do the cooking and serving, bhai.' Or it was, 'Hai hai, it's so hot, I'll melt if I don't have the AC running full blast, let's get together at my place.' Of course it was often true, it was very hot in her flat and even though they consciously kept the fare simple, it still bothered her to have to buy the pre-packaged biscuits instead of the usual cheap bakery ones she kept for herself. Then, often the others had some non-veg item and she could only ever afford simple veg things. She resented their coming but resented even more their reluctance to come.

She felt tired and frazzled and broken by the time the meet was over at her house, but still, it didn't seem right that Sheila should just not turn up at her house. That morning, again, Tosh called to say that Sheila could not come, something about her husband. Well, it always was about her husband, wasn't it? My husband this, my husband that. I mean, these women had to realize they were individuals too. How could such nicely brought up, decently educated women be so wound up in their husband's lives? It was just one outing in the week, let the husband manage!

Satya promised herself not to say anything, but felt her irritation simmering inside herself and that always gave her acidity which in turn led to a headache. She rubbed some balm onto her temples and covered up the biscuits with a clean duster. She didn't have many napkins left. A few years ago, Kunti had presented her with a set of napkins, but Satya had really minded it and had said so. She remembered that altercation clearly, even now: 'Oh, how lovely, Kunti behen, napkins! I'm sure you must have noticed that I don't have any fancy ones myself, hain na?'

'Arrey, what do you mean, Satya? I just saw these really pretty ones in the Ashoka Hotel lobby. Some nuns were selling embroidered stuff. I just thought you'd like them.'

'Like them? Like them – or need them? Come on Kunti, admit it, you have been uncomfortable using paper tissues or the home embroidered hand towels that I use, that's the truth, na?' She had tried to laugh, but she knew that she was sounding as bitter and old-maidish as she really, in truth, was. No one talked about it and no one ever presented her with napkins again, although she had really loved using the delicately embroidered napkins, with a spray of tiny pansies in soft colours. But she wouldn't, couldn't admit that she'd like another set now. So she hunted out a clean chequered duster which would pass off as a napkin, to cover the food. She clicked her tongue and flapped in vain at the flies that invaded her cramped little lobby that served as a living room, staring yet again at the durrie with its curling corners that tried, in vain, to cover the DDA grey cement floor. Why did they have to make everything in such depressing shades? She had been to Kerala once, accompanying a group from the Geography department. She was so delighted with their cheery red floors. The same cement, really, just with some imaginative red colour mixed in so that it looked so smart and clean. This floor looked unswept, no matter how many times she hounded the cleaning woman and made her mop it over and over.

With one of her famous exaggerated sighs, she looked around, letting out a large, acidic burp. Everything was ready, or at least as ready as it would be. She was getting impatient, although the clock showed that it was not yet time for their get-together.

Finally, Tosh and Kunti arrived together. They had been to the tailor that morning and only talked about the blouses they had got stitched.

'Such a chor, this tailor, I tell you, ate up half the cloth I'd given and trying to pass off this tiny blouse as though it was ever going to fit me.'

'Arrey, all tailors are the same, you should ask them how much cloth and get just a little less than that.'

'I'm thinking of getting those knitted blouses for winter. They stretch also, so you can adjust very easily.'

They clambered up, huffing and puffing, to the third-floor flat. By the first floor, though, they had to stop chatting as they needed to conserve their breath for the climb ahead. By the second floor, they needed to stop for a break.

'Hai, how does Satya do this every day?'

'Sometimes twice a day!'

'I swear, how does she do this?'

'Main te mar gayi!'

'She must find it easier because she is not fat like us.'

'Maybe that's why she is so slim and trim, this is the world's best exercise!'

'You mean that all people living on the third floor are slim?'

'Maybe that's why they're called "flats" – because everyone in them is flat!'

Laughing and gasping for breath, they finally made it to the flat and collapsed in heaps of sweaty, heaving laughter. 'By God, Satya, how do you do this trek every day? I swear, I take my hat off to you! You live on Mt Everest,' laughed Kunti, mopping her brow with a delicately perfumed handkerchief.

Seeing Satya's face, Tosh immediately realized she was not enjoying this, so she quickly tried to change the topic, 'Hat, Kunti? What hat will you take off? You don't wear a hat!' she giggled jovially at her feeble joke, hoping it would head off any comment-baazi between the two. But a pre-irritated Satya was too much on the edge to let it go. In a quiet, bitter voice, she said, 'I do it because I have to, Kunti Behenji, not because I like to. I don't have anyone who will buy a ground floor place for me. Just because I don't grumble, doesn't mean ...,' her bitter tone was edged with tears, ' ... if you find it so hard, maybe you shouldn't come to my flat anymore!'

Her outburst brought the laughter to an abrupt halt.

'Satya, Satya, arrey, of course I didn't mean it like that, you know that, my sister, don't be like that, na? I am full of admiration for you, I was really only laughing at myself, not at you, you know that! I was laughing at how unfit I am, how overweight and complimenting you, only ...'

Satya's back straightened, and Tosh and Kunti held their breaths, not sure whether this was going to blow over or get worse. But then she slumped, shoulders unbending from their aggressive stance. 'I know, I know, I'm sorry, that's not what I meant either, I just, you know … I feel bad because when it is my turn, one or the other won't turn up, that's all. Like today, look, now Sheila is not here.'

'But Satya, it has nothing to do with it being at your place. She would not have been able to attend, no matter where it was.'

'I know, but I still wish that you all would make the effort of being here more regularly, see, maybe it's only a coincidence, but every time it's at my place, someone can't come. Last time it was you, Toshji, this time it's Sheila.'

'Last time I had a touch of fever, Satya and this time, well, you know how it is with Sheila. Her husband has been sinking and things have taken a turn for the worse. Of course she has to be with him now, we must understand that.'

'I know, I know, of course I know. But sometimes I feel, you know, bad.'

'Chalo, bhai, let's not spend more time now feeling bad-shad, let's play, na!' said Kunti, who was always a bit impatient with Satya, but careful to keep her tone mild and cheerfully friendly, lest Satya start off again, as she was wont to do.

They had switched to playing rummy a couple of years ago when their group started having problems making up a bridge foursome. One or the other invariably had some preoccupation and was unable to make it. It had caused them some grief at having their game disrupted, and then Tosh, ever the one with the calm touch, had come up with this utterly simple and obvious solution. They could just play some other game. And so rummy it was. It could be played with four or three or even just two of them.

The game proceeded now, happily. Kunti won the first hand and then Satya won the next three which chuffed her up and brightened her mood.

When they decided to take their tea break and Satya put the kettle on to boil, they called Sheila to find out how things were with her. They called from Tosh's mobile as she was the only one who knew how to use the speaker facility. This way, they could all be a part of the conversation. But the news was not good.

'I don't know, I just don't know, the doctors are expecting he will slip into a deeper coma. They asked if they should put him onto life support systems or take him into intensive care in a hospital, but Annu and I have decided no. There's no good to be achieved in making him suffer more, is there? He is not going to become better, so why prolong his suffering ....'

'So then?'

'I – I don't know, they say it won't be long ... now ...,' her voice broke. The others looked at each other. What was there to say?

'I don't know if I'm making the right choice, or have I made the decision for my own selfish motives?'

No, no, they all assured her, of course, it was a difficult decision, but the only correct one.

'But, but I feel so terribly, terribly guilty. I can't help thinking that if it had been the other way around, he would have kept me alive. I know that. He would have done everything, everything to keep me alive, no matter what. So then, why am I letting him ... go ... die?' She broke down and wept, having spoken the terrible word at last. The three friends on the other side of the phone line could only look helplessly at each other. What was there to say?

It was a somber group, then, that sat down to the tea and biscuits. Unconsciously, Satya dipped her biscuits into the tea and bit into the soggy biscuit. It brought back her childhood, the days that were comforting and safe and there were no terrible decisions to take. She felt grateful, suddenly, she had no one close enough to take such a decision for.

'I think it won't be long now. Her husband will slip away in a few days.'

'Hai, poor thing, poor Sheila.'

'In a way, it will be a relief for her, don't you think?'

'A relief yes, she has had to look after him for so long, in this state.'

'But you know, it will be very difficult for her too. Her whole life has revolved around looking after him like an infant for so long. Suddenly, she will feel a terrible void when he is no longer there.'

'Especially in that huge house of hers, she is going to get very lonely there, no?'

'What will she do with the house, has she said anything?'

'Do? What do you mean, do?'

'You mean, you think she should continue to live there?'

'Then what?'

'Bhai, it's such a huge place ... do you think she should stay there, all on her own?'

'She's been staying there practically on her own all this time, I don't think she'll want to change it; why, it's the house she and her husband built together, I don't think she'll want to leave the place.'

'Yes, I can understand that. Sentiment-shentiment and all that, phir bhi, living in a place like that, sprawling, with only servants ... I don't know, I wouldn't like it.'

'But what else can she do, no?'

'Maybe she could take in some paying guests, you know.'

'Hai, hai, no, you never know what kind of people come. I've heard now there are even terrorists who come in and stay as tenants and all. I don't think it will be safe.'

'She can take in only girl students.'

'It's a huge responsibility no? And girls nowadays, I know what they're like you know, being a teacher for so many years. Now, these modern girls are so badmash, fast, you know.'

'Oh ho, they're not all like that!'

'How can you tell which one is and which one isn't, they'll be all decent when they come for the interview – they'll wear salwar-kameez and all. And then – who knows what they're up to in their inny-minni skirts, with their boyfriends and god knows what!'

'Then what? Maybe she could sell to one of these builders ...'

'Hain, that may not be too bad. After all, you hear of so many people nowadays who are selling their old house and then buying something in Gurgaon or Noida and having a lot of money to spend and save in case of illness or whatever. That may be a good option.'

'But you know these builders, they're such badmashes, I tell you, it's like a mafia, a builder mafia. Especially with old people, they promise something, but they take you for a real jolly ride.'

' ... and Gurgaon, Noida, that's too far out. Can't move so far when we're used to being close to everything, na?'

'There's also the other thing to do, one of my colleagues has done this. You know, you give the place to the builder and they put you up somewhere else, like a flat or something. They pay your rent and everything for the one year it takes to build the place. Once it is ready, you get to keep one or even two of the flats and the rest they sell. That may not be bad. Paisey bhi aur ghar bhi in the same place.'

'Hai, baba, I feel very unsafe, banni banayee cheez ko, kissi stranger ke haath mein de do, I don't know. These builders-shilders are very fishy people.'

'But she can't just be there on her own you know.'

'I don't know why you're making such a big thing out of it, you know. As I said, she practically lives there on her own already. It's not as if her husband could actually do anything if something were to happen.'

'Phir bhi, aaj kal ke zamane mein – all on her own ... People out there get to know there's a senior citizen lady living on her own, you know ... I feel it's not right.'

'She'll never go and live with her daughter and son-in-law, she's said as much.'

'Bhai, I think we should get over this rubbish now. I mean, yeh koi zamana hai that we can't go and live with our daughters, just because society says so?'

'Phir bhi, tradition is tradition, na?'

'Kya tradition? Look, I go and live with my daughter and no problem ...'

'Your daughter is married to a man who is really a firang na? He's just an Indian in name, being born and brought up in the US – so of course it is not a problem for them.'

'Oh ho, this was a tradition when we were girls. Now, there's none of this tradition-vadition. Of course she can go and stay with her daughter.'

'Nahin bhai, I don't think it's only a question of tradition and girls, even if she had a son, I would still say why lose your independence? Ask me, I would much rather be on my own than be a glorified ayah in my son's house, and also feel obliged to them for having me.'

'You say that now, Kunti,' Satya butted in predictably, 'but try living on your own. It's not easy, you know, not easy at all. Look what happened to you when they just had to go for a few days. You had a panic attack.'

'Oh ho, that was different. You just have to get used to these things.'

And then, suddenly, like a dam bursting, Satya practically exploded, 'What we have to learn is to give up these stupid traditions that have no meaning. It was one thing saying you could not go to your daughter's marital home when she was not working and totally dependent on her husband. But in today's day and age, why would my parents not come to stay with me, tell me, why? Why couldn't you come?'

She was as startled as the others with this outburst. Satya rubbed her eyes and forced the image of her parents from them. She looked up to reassure herself that these were her friends here and only her friends.

Slowly the story came out. Satya's mother had cancer and her father had refused to come and stay with his daughter despite the fact he was completely helpless without his wife. 'He couldn't even make a cup of tea for himself!' There were better medical facilities in Delhi than in Gwalior, it would have been more convenient for all concerned, but no, they could not come to her. 'It's not as though I was dependent on anyone. I was living off my own salary. In fact, maybe I could have saved some money if I did not have to take so many unpaid leaves and travel up and down, up and down. I almost lost my job with the amount of leave I had to take. But bas, it was tradition, so, whether I would have been so happy to have the chance to look after my parents, whether it was the most practical decision ... they would not come to stay with me and that was that!' Even after her mother died despite the chemo and radiation, her father was adamant. He had a nasty old maid to look after him and with his failing eyesight, could not even see she was robbing him blind! 'She was stealing things I should have inherited. Things that would have helped me in my life. But no – they would rather be robbed by a stranger than come to me.'

'You are right Satya, I think we have to try and change our way of thinking. But ....' Tosh sighed, 'I don't think she will want to stay with Annu.'

It was an old argument, one they'd been through a thousand times before, but also one that they never seemed to tire of. It was the issue closest to their hearts: their immediate futures, insecure each in their own ways. They did not have a very long future ahead; they were, after all, in their late sixties. Tosh had celebrated her seventieth birthday last year, the others were not far behind. And each of them was leading a life less than what she had imagined her sunset years would be.

6

Two mornings later, the phone lines were abuzz. Sheila's husband had passed away. Tosh picked up Kunti, who, of course, set off on her grumbling immediately. She could never get the car and driver when she needed it, not even for an occasion like this. Satya sniffed out of the window, creating a little cloud on the air-conditioned window-pane, feeling offended she did not even have a driver and only a beaten up old car to drive: so, technically, she had the greatest right to grumble, but she was too good to do so. Tosh took in all of it, but she felt too sad and weary to take them on just yet. So she looked away, drawn back to her own husband's funeral. To the thoughts that were never far away, and indeed, easily conjured, with so much talk of Sheila's imminent loss. She had not worn her kajal this morning for she knew there would be tears. She smiled quietly to herself, remembering what her husband had said on their wedding night. She cried all through the ceremony, then even harder at the bidai and of course, on the long drive from her house to her new home. Her kohl spread into big dark circles around her eyes and her husband had laughed and said that he thought he was marrying a beautiful girl, but was tricked into marrying a panda bear!

They arrived at Sheila's home and drove up the big driveway, the kind that did not exist in modern homes in Delhi anymore. The rambling garden was faded and unkempt, the mistress of the house being too preoccupied to tend to it. It looked sad and decrepit, as though it too had suffered a loss, as though it too faced an uncertain future. They took their chappals off at the threshold, noting that there were not too many others.

The body was laid white and stiff, cold, surrounded by ice and icy white flowers. The air was heavy and smoky with agarbatti and dhoop.

A CD of bhajans played a tad loudly. A single diya flickered near the cotton-wool stoppered head. Next to the body – the body – sat Sheila looking old, much much older than they had seen her just a week ago. Her skin was paper thin and she seemed blanched of all colour. They rushed forward as she tried to get up on seeing them. She had been sitting too long. She swayed and had to be helped into a chair. She seemed to have cried herself dry and now looked just drained. Finished.

The friends stroked her hands, her bent head, her weary back. She nodded in acknowledgement and gratitude for their solicitude but had no strength to say anything. And there was nothing more to be said.

One by one they consoled Annu – Sheila's daughter – and her husband, Sonjoy. Annu was crying quietly and continuously. Sonjoy was trying to busy himself with the jobs on hand. There weren't too many people there to help. He hoped that someone would help console his wife as well. Finally he went over to the group of friends. They patted his back and told him what he already knew, what he had known for a long time now: that all the responsibility was now on his shoulders. He told them that he needed to go and make the arrangements for the funeral. Would they hold the fort for a bit. He turned to go, then again he turned back to them, having glanced, yet again, at the pitiful aloneness of his wife. 'Please,' he appealed, 'please, get Annu to drink some tea or something, she ... you see, and she's refusing to eat or drink anything ...'

'Don't worry, beta, you leave it to us.'

'Wait, tell me what needs to be done. I will call my secretary, Panditji, he knows how to handle these things, just wait ...'

Panditji was Tosh's faithful Man Friday, he was her husband's secretary and now retired, he enjoyed helping his Bibiji as often as possible. He stood in queues to pay her tax, electricity and water bills. He got her car serviced when needed. There was nothing as vulgar as a salary between them, but Tosh paid for his granddaughter's education and she had presented the daughter with jewellery when she was to be married. She called him now and he was there within the hour, having brought with him a bag of flower petals, a havan kund, samagri, mauli, sandal wood and a bier. He quietly took over the proceedings; being a Pandit, he would conduct the ceremony himself. Annu's husband was grateful for all this being taken off his hands, for in truth, he knew nothing about all this. So he stood beside his wife and she leaned on him.

And then it was over, Sheila's husband was finally consigned to the flames and a date was fixed three days later for the chautha. As the subdued group prepared to leave, Annu came up to them. There was a new problem. How was she to leave her mother alone while she and her husband took the ashes to Haridwar? 'I don't want to go there and come back all in one day,' she said, 'I'd like to stay one night, but mama ....'

It was then that Satya came up with the solution. Tentatively she offered, 'You know, I could come and stay with her while you're away,' she laughed her self-depreciating laugh. 'There's no one to miss me at home you know, except, maybe the doodhwala!'

The others all congratulated her on her selfless loyalty to her friend, though of course, they were all also aware that it was not completely selfless. After Kunti's and Tosh's night together, it had been an appealing and tempting thought in Satya's mind all along.

'It's no problem really,' she assured the grieving daughter, 'it is a pleasure for me to be able to be of use to someone, not be totally useless all the time.'

So, despite Sheila's teary assurances she would be fine, that she had to learn to live on her own now, it was decided Satya would come later in the evening to stay with her friend. Mentally, though, Satya was fretting about her nightwear, knowing that her fraying, faded kaftans were too shabby to wear in company. Perhaps a quick trip to Lajpat Nagar or Sarojini Nagar to indulge in one new one was in order. Despite the solemnity of the occasion, Satya couldn't help the lifting of her heart, a surge of relief, or was it happiness?

She would not sleep alone that night.

7

Annu and her husband left after many anxious words of advice. Sheila assured them she would be all right. That she was just so tired all she wanted just then was to sleep. Yes she was sleepy; it was a long, long time since she had had a comfortable night of undisturbed sleep. She had been getting up twice, thrice at night to look in on her husband. Now all she wanted was a dreamless sleep. Annu made her promise she would not try to do any sorting and tidying up by herself. Again Sheila assured her and, of course, Satya would be there later in the evening. Sheila found putting up a brave face exhausting work. She needed to let her guard down now and grieve openly.

She was always the stronger one who pitched in with physical work whenever it was needed. In fact, when she fell ill once, quite seriously, he got into quite a flap about it, wondering how he could ever manage without her. He made her promise to let him be the first to die, because he was sure she would be all right without him. When she protested, he said, 'Oh I know you'll miss me, but, don't you see, I would die without you. And promise me yet one more thing – if I die before you, I don't want you to live the life of a grieving widow. You have to enjoy life.'

And she had kept her promise. But she was feeling so much like a grieving widow now. Like when her parents had died, she'd really felt orphaned: although she was in her forties, she was still an orphan.

As the others left, and once her daughter left the house, Sheila told the servants to go and have a rest too. They had already put the furniture back in place, swept the place clean of samagri and flower petals. Reluctantly, they left. They were tired, but yet they wondered whether one of them should stay back with memsahib. No, she assured them, she'd like to be alone for a while and she only wanted to sleep.

And now she was alone in the house at last. She wandered around alone. The house was deathly still. She had thought she would just go right off to sleep, but now that she was alone, with not one thing to do, sleep fled her eyes. It was quiet, oh so quiet. She noticed the air was no longer filled with sounds of her husband's laboured breathing. She had not realized how omnipresent it was or how acutely her ears had got attuned to listening for that sound.

Like a ghost, she walked through the living room which had become a death room after her husband's body lay there. She gasped, the floor was still icy cold from all the ice he lay on. No warmth. She moved onto a carpet. Then suddenly the memory of how they had bought it came rushing back. It was a long time ago, when money was not easy to come by. The year wintered early and they needed a carpet. The floor was so bare and cold. A carpet-seller had trundled his cart by just the other day. They'd seen a good, cheap carpet that went just right with their deep green sofa upholstery. But they didn't have the money to spare.

They rummaged around and got out everything that was disposable – stacks of old newspapers, cartons of things long out of use, old fans and cooler pumps, stabilizers and the like. Then they called in their kabbadiwala. He offered them, oh not too much money. They knew it would not be enough for a carpet. But then the kabbadiwala asked if they had a full length mirror. He had just got married and his wife wanted a full length mirror – if they had one to spare, he would pay a decent price for it. Sheila had one, the one she used to tie her saris in front of. Her husband said there was no need to sell it; they would find the money somehow. But she was insistent; she got the mirror taken off her bedroom cupboard door and now they had enough money to buy their carpet. And she never had that mirror replaced, but became adept at tying her saris mirror-less, even after there was enough money to buy many more.

After that they always had to choose green upholstery even though they once loved a blue! She sat on the broad sofa that had been her husband's bed when he first fell ill. He wanted to be in the living room, instead of stuck in the bedroom. Even when he sunk into a coma and she brought him back from the hospital, she kept him in the living room. It was as he wanted. Although the doctors said he would sink further into the coma and eventually slip away, she thought if he did wake up, he would be where he had first chosen to be.

She lay down on the green sofa, snuggling into the cushions. She hoped sleep would overcome her. But her mind was restless; there had never been a time she had nothing to do. She had never slept in the afternoons. So now, although her mind and body were exhausted, she got up again and resumed her wandering. Every corner, every nook held precious memories: things bought together, things gifted to each other on occasions or sometimes 'just like that', for the love of each other. Precious, precious things. Each imbued with significance and love.

Aimlessly wandering around tired her out. She needed to find something to do. Something significant and useful, so she did not feel like a ghost, as though she herself was dead. Lost, fettered here while her husband flew off to an unknown destination.

She needed something to do. She was not used to idle hands. Her upbringing always drilled into her that idle hands were, after all, the devil's workshop. She was always doing something, whether it was knitting, embroidery, polishing the brass and silver, something ... something to be counted in the world of the living.

Her wanderings took her to her bedroom – now her bedroom, not theirs, just hers. Even though her husband had not used this room for a long time now, it had still been 'their' room. But now ... she stood before her husband's cupboard – looking at it at first, then reaching out, touching the handle. She did not dare to open it. Not yet. She wasn't ready to see his clothes hanging uselessly just yet. She turned away and sat on the trunk that served as a window seat. She leaned against the coolness of the window pane and realized her forehead was burning hot. She fingered the soft velvet of the bedspread covering the trunk and felt herself sinking into despair. 'No,' she struggled against the tide of tears, 'No!' she must do something. Without stopping to put concrete thought into it, she pulled the velvet cover off the trunk. It pooled in a blood-red puddle of folds at her feet. She sank onto it and opened the trunk with the key that was always hidden under the cover. The padlock gave way arthritically and she lifted the trunk lid to reveal winter clothes. Yes, she told herself, I'll start here. She pulled the clothes out, trying to sort them to make some sense of them. At first she made a pile of her own clothes and another of his: lingering over the left over smell of her husband – a strange, tobacco-ey smell she had never liked, but was terrified of losing now. And then she came across her own brightly coloured sweaters, cardigans and shawls. Turquoise blue, emerald green, the parrot green her husband's sister had once gifted her and she had politely worn though it was not the sort of colour she could ever carry off. Jewel bright colours, sparkling and frivolous. She could not, rather would not, wear them anymore. Although her husband hated her wearing pale clothes, she must now don widow's weeds, mustn't she? Surely she could not wear these colours. So she started another pile, this time of clothes she would have to discard. Perhaps her daughter would like some. She pulled out the good tweed coat her husband would wear on formal occasions. It was one of the first things he bought for himself when he started travelling abroad. It was very good quality and it would be a pity to waste it. Should she offer it to her son-in-law? Would he mind? Would it embarrass him, forcing him to wear something he might not be comfortable wearing – much like the parrot green sweater? Well, she'd ask her daughter; it just seemed such a shame to discard a perfectly good thing like an imported tweed coat. The trunk was emptying out, the piles were tottering when she came to her wedding jora and his sherwani, folded into muslin and neem leaves. Her old fingers hesitated on the fabric and then slowly, slowly, she reached in and drew her wedding clothes out. Tenderly she unwrapped the Banarasi brocade sari, the impossibly tiny brocade blouse that seemed to have been stitched for a doll – she smiled, finding it hard to imagine she was ever so petite. The satin of her petticoat felt cool and sexy, she shuddered with the remembered pleasure of her wedding night. How gentle he had been, how concerned, how loving. How his hands caressed her legs through the silky satin of the petticoat. He had painstakingly taken the flowers out of her hair, all those pins that held up the joora were snagging on her hair-sprayed hair. But he gently prised each one off, even when she told him he could leave them, he said, 'No, how will you sleep with such a helmet of pins in your hair?' They laughed then and he slid his hand up her arms and cupped her face and kissed her for the first time.

He would never kiss her again. It was a long, long time since they had kissed; he had sunk so, gone so far away from her, deep into his illness, long before he died. But he'd still been there, still been the central focus of her life. The centre around which her universe revolved. That's why she felt so aimless and rootless now, her axis had fallen away, she had nothing to revolve around anymore.

Fresh tears fell onto the muslin-embraced sherwani. Hurriedly she wiped them off. She did not want it stained with her loss. Tenderly, oh so lovingly, she unwrapped the white cloth and traced the trellis design of gold thread on the raw silk. Unfolding it, she saw that a crack was growing in the fabric, she should hang it up so that the crease did not go too deep. As she struggled up, her sari fell onto the floor, in a cascade of bright red. She hesitated: which should she attend to first? Then she decided; leaving the sari, she lovingly carried the sherwani to his cupboard and pulled out a big coat hanger. She opened the top button and slipped the hanger in, her hands rubbing longingly on the inside of the silk-lined collar, the part lucky enough to have rested on his skin. She hooked the hanger onto her cupboard door and went back to the sari.

Picking up the blouse first, she held it up in wonder: it really was doll-like. Could she even get a sleeve on now? She slipped her hand through the sleeve, and pulled it up her arm. It got stuck just above the elbow. No, not even a sleeve! She laughed despite her sorrow, then wondered if the petticoat would fit; that was so small too. She stepped into the soft satin. It was tight around the hips, but that was also because she had her salwar on. So she pulled off the salwar and tried, once again, to get into the petticoat. She loved the feel of the satin on her bare legs, wondering why she had started getting the thick cotton ones instead, this was so much nicer. There, it was on, she did not need to tie the nara, her belly held the petticoat up. Now she bent down to pick up the sari. The gorgeous golden peacocks on the palla danced as she started to fold up the sari. Then on a whim, she tucked her kameez up and began to wrap the sari around her, the pleats falling into place, as though they longed to do so. She covered her head with the pallav, then, bride-like, demurely turned and stepped towards the cupboard where the sherwani awaited its bride.

She looked down, but stole a coy glance at her husband, smiling, demure. When she reached it, she lifted both her hands, as though holding a jaimala. Her hands rested on her husband's shoulders. She rested her head on his chest, then put her arms around his waist, lifting his hand onto her own shoulder in an embrace. She looked up at him and giggled, flushed, as the empty sleeve brushed her breast as it fell away. She slipped her hand up and naughtily opened two buttons of the sherwani and slid her hand in.

She gasped. She was shocked, shocked to find it was empty. There was no husband there, never would be again. Horrified, she stepped away and caught a glimpse of herself in her bridal sari. And then she burst into tears. Loud, wailing tears, not the quiet, dignified, graceful ones. Now there was no one to be brave for. She broke down, howling like a wounded dog. She hugged the pillow to stem the loneliness and to absorb the pain and cries. Keening with whimpering sobs, she rocked herself into a deep sleep.

She dreamt of her wedding, red flowers all around. But everyone was dressed in white, except she and she shouted at them, *Why are you in white, it's my wedding! How dare you? Take off your clothes of mourning!* She screamed. They looked at her with pity in their eyes. *Why are you looking at me like that?*

The baraat arrived, a cheerful shehnai struck up; the band marched on leading the way for the bridegroom. She rushed out to put the jaimala on her husband, but his clothes were empty. Only his clothes had come for the wedding – where was her husband? Why was he not there? Bells were ringing at the wedding mandap, temple bells, clanging, louder, more insistent.

Sheila awoke in a sweat, but the bells kept jangling persistently, even when she realized she was awake. It was the front doorbell, ringing insistently, urgently. Someone was at the door, could it be her husband, returned at last? She rushed to the door.

8

Satya gasped. She had expected to find a widow dressed in white; instead, here was her friend, sensible, down-to-earth Sheila, dressed in her bridal sari and a kurta underneath.

'Sheila – what on earth?' Satya stammered, then hurriedly looked around outside, hoping no one else had witnessed this sight. This vulgar, inappropriate sight. She pushed Sheila in and quickly shut the door behind her. She turned on her friend, her disapproval evident. 'Sheila, what do you think you're doing? Yeh sab kya hai?'

Sheila, not quite understanding what the matter was, still carrying in her eyes the remnants of her confusing dream, looked puzzled. She could not even place Satya correctly. She seemed familiar, but, but who was she exactly? And why was she so angry? Satya was appalled to see Sheila look at her like that, blankly without recognition. 'Sheila, Sheila, listen, come, come, sit down ... you, you're not well.' As always, Satya wished Tosh behenji was here. She'd know what to do. It was obvious Sheila's sorrow had cut her too deep. She was unable to cope with it.

She led Sheila like a child towards the sofa, soon realizing it was the husband's deathbed; so she turned her and headed her towards another armchair. Like a child, Sheila allowed herself to be led, not resisting, not comprehending. Just following, until Satya started to take off the sari.

'Arrey, what are you doing? I'm not supposed to ....' Then she looked at Satya with a glimmer of recognition, she looked around. And Satya knew she had come back to the present. She watched Sheila look down at herself with an expression of surprise, then horror on her face. 'How ...?'

Gently, gently, Satya pulled the sari off. She saw that she was in a petticoat and looked around, spotted the salwar lying abandoned and handed it back to Sheila. 'Here, now don't worry, just change, then I'll make us some tea. Here, take it na, it'll be all right.'

She looked away as Sheila pulled the petticoat off obediently. Satya couldn't resist and stole a glance at Sheila's plump thighs and rounded buttocks. Her own were thin and shriveled like old raisins or plums left on the plate too long. The juice had leaked out of them long ago – if there ever had been any!

As soon as she was done, Satya got Sheila into bed, blindsiding her protests. Sheila was quite relieved not to have to do anything. Not to have to decide, or be in charge. She had a strange feeling of disconnectedness, as though she was watching herself on television. She closed her eyes and found they were burning.

Satya went into the kitchen. She was not very comfortable here; hers was a very simple one, everything in its place, where she knew it would be. She did not know what exactly she would do. Luckily Kunti promised to send food over. As there had been a death, there would be no cooking in this house for a few days. Satya just needed to make tea, but that was daunting enough. She stood in the middle of the kitchen, wringing her hands. She wished she'd had the sense to cook something at home and bring it in a tiffin-carrier.

Water, yes, first Sheila should have some water to drink. That was a start. She filled a glass from the water filter. She realized that she was thirsty too, so she got one for herself as well. Sheila stirred as Satya walked in, 'Oh good, I'm so thirsty, my throat is parched,' she almost moaned. She drank and Satya stroked her head a little awkwardly. Her head was hot. Satya felt her forehead: she was definitely running a fever. Oh dear, this was not the evening she'd had in mind. Somehow, despite the circumstance, she'd hoped for a Tosh-Kunti type of sleepover.

Eventually, Satya managed to find some Crocin and a soft towel to sponge Sheila down. She rang Kunti who was in a mess of her own. The food was made: alu, puri and some vegetables, but her driver was missing. He was not answering his cell phone. 'Patta nahin kahan mar gaya hai, and I'd told him that he had to deliver the food to Sheila's, now see, he's disappeared. So unreliable these people are.'

'Doesn't matter, what can you do?' Satya tried to sound more confident than she was feeling. She told Tosh about it. Tosh offered to send some khichdi over. Yes, that was a good idea, Satya was relieved she wouldn't have to figure things out in the kitchen. She sat by Sheila, stroking her head and massaging her tired, burning feet.

Then Tosh called: her driver had gone off duty. He was out of his house now and not carrying his cell phone. She did not know when he'd be back. There was no way for her to deliver the khichdi. Satya felt faintly annoyed; it was wrong to light the kitchen fire on the day of a death. Although she knew that it was nobody's fault, she felt at a loss herself. Tosh also told her not to worry, she was confident Sheila would enjoy whatever Satya could rustle up for her. After a reassuring 'good night', Tosh left Satya to it.

'All right,' Satya gritted her teeth, 'I can do this, of course I can.' Luckily it wasn't Tosh's very fancy new modular kitchen. 'If I had to do this there, I'd *really* panic!' She smiled. She managed to find the rice, although she was unsure whether to use the good basmati or the cheaper parmal. Then she was confused whether to use ghee or the sunflower oil. She soaked the dal and rice, and hunted for the utensils to make the khichdi. She couldn't find any matches anywhere. It was one of those new types of stoves with an automatic lighter, but you had to press the button and turn the knob at the same time and Satya was terrified of leaving the gas on too long.

Finally, she found a match box in the living room, next to a candle stand (so efficient!). There, now the khichdi was on. She decided to make it with the more expensive rice and the ghee, to give it more taste and flavour. She was feeling pleased with herself. She had accomplished something with quite a lot of ease. She need not have been so worried. As she flung in some whole spices for flavour, she knew that she would not be so nervous the next time.

Although she was weak and tired and feverish, Sheila obeyed Satya's instructions to eat a little. Sheila smiled up at her, 'It's very tasty, I didn't know you were such a good cook!' Satya was pleased; she always got biscuits and snacks from outside when she had the rummy mornings at her house, because she never felt sure enough about her own abilities. But here, here she'd managed to make something in an unfamiliar kitchen and even made poor, dear Sheila smile.

After dinner Satya got quite a kick out of leaving the used dishes in the sink, soaking, awaiting servants in the morning. She'd never had that luxury herself and sometimes she would be so tired at the end of the day and yet still do the dishes. She told herself she hated leaving the kitchen dirty and that it attracted cockroaches, but the fact was she knew she'd have to do it the next morning anyhow, and so she might as well do it before everything dried to a crust.

Sheila told her that she could sleep in the guest bedroom. She assured her that she was used to sleeping alone since her husband could not be moved from his sofa. But Satya noticed a wistfulness in her eye and she offered to sleep in the same room with Sheila. They chatted as they lay in the big soft bed. Sheila told her about her life with her husband, the love, the sharing. How caring he was.

Satya listened with awe. This was a life she knew nothing about. How would it have been for her? Sheila asked, 'How did you manage, Satya, all by yourself? It's so brave of you. You know, when it was certain that my Narenderji did not have long to go, I started worrying, wondering how I was going to manage my life ... Then I would look to you for inspiration.'

'Me? You'd look to me for inspiration? Arrey, who is more competent than you, Sheila? Look, not only have you managed, but managed everything so beautifully and looked after your husband for so long, so well – its no mean feat. In fact, you are an inspiration for us. We all have to learn from you.'

'Well, look at you, how much you have had to do on your own. Until Narenderji fell ill, I hardly had to lift a finger at all, you know, income tax, property tax, getting this house converted to free hold, arrey, there were thousands of things that I did not know anything about, I still don't.'

'Don't worry; you have your daughter and son-in-law to help you out with these things.'

'I know, thank god for them, but that's just my point, na. From one, I can now depend on the others, but you've always done it all on your own, I can't even begin to tell you how much I admire that.'

Satya almost blushed. She was that pleased. She tried to minimize the compliment by saying she led such a simple life, there was hardly anything to manage really. She was so unused to talking about herself she quickly diverted the topic back to Sheila.

'How come you never had more than your one daughter, Sheila? Didn't your husband, your in-laws want you to have a son?'

'My in-laws, yes, of course, Naren is, was ... WAS, hai, how hard that is to say ...,' she stopped, swallowing at the hard lump of 'was' in her throat, then continued softly, sadly. 'Naren was the only son and his parents wanted a grandson very badly, there was quite a lot of pressure on me.'

'And Narenderji?'

'That's the thing, you know I had a very hard pregnancy and the labour, oh, it was the worst, went on for three full days. So much pain and in those days they would not just do a caesarian the way they would now. How much I cried, I can't tell you. So after Annu was born, Naren swore, never, never again was I to have another pregnancy. After some years, I really wanted to have another baby, I always felt so close to my own sister and I wanted my daughter to have that too, but no, Naren said if I had to go through that kind of pain again, he would die, he could not bear it. And so, we just had the one daughter. We even thought of adopting a baby from an orphanage, but my in-laws were so against it and I knew it would lead to fights, or Annu being favoured over the adopted one, so I just dropped it. But believe me, she's been more than any son could have been, she is just ....'

'I know, you're lucky to have her, at least one ....' Satya could not mask the pain of never having a child of her own. 'How did it happen, Satya? How come you never got married? Was there someone in your life ever?' Sheila was not one to ask personal questions, but she could sense Satya's need to talk about it.

And she was right. It was a secret burden Satya had borne all her life. She started her story without hesitation, though the remembered shame crept up, choking her.

'There was a boy. One who my family had found through their own network. He came with his parents to meet me. I was nervous and excited. I walked in after they had settled into our drawing room to find this handsome man looking at me. I could have fainted. I wanted to say "yes, yes, yes" right away. It was love at first sight for me! I sat next to him and he asked me the usual questions. I thought he had "yes" in his eyes too.

Satya's nails were digging into her palms, but she was used to hiding this from others. The shame rose like bile within her. Sheila, the patient, waited.

'And then, suddenly, unannounced, uninvited, Meera came. My most beautiful cousin. She burst in on the scene – looking radiant. She'd come to tell us that she'd topped her university exams. And ... and I lost my prospective husband right there. I saw the look in his eyes as they fell upon Meera. I knew his "no" was on the way. I knew that he wanted to marry her instead.

'Meera was apologetic and all. Of course it wasn't her fault. And she'd certainly not intended this to happen. But he was besotted with her. He said he'd marry her and no one else. She refused him. She wouldn't do such a thing to me. But it was too late. I never met him again.'

'And you never met anyone else.'

'Oh no!' Satya shivered, 'I forbade my parents from ever making me go through that again. I couldn't expose myself to that kind of humiliation. I swore that I'd be independent – lead a life by myself, for myself. But,' she added with a sigh, 'I still think of him sometimes and wonder what my life would have been like if Meera hadn't come that afternoon.'

Sheila reached out and held her hand. The bereaved consoling the consoler.

And gradually, they fell into a sweet sleep.

The next morning they awoke early, as dawn was just breaking. Satya woke up first. She was startled by the unfamiliar bedside table that met her eyes as they opened groggily. Then she turned towards her still sleeping friend and could barely contain the rush of warm happiness, like liquid golden honey pouring into her. She'd never woken up in bed with another person before. She didn't jump out of bed as she usually did, flinging herself into the bustle of the day. This morning she lingered, enjoying the warm breathing of her friend, looking at her until she awoke and smiled at her. It had been a while since Sheila too had slept in the same bed as someone. But she was glad that on her first husband-less day she had a friend to share the bed, or rather the first waking moments, with.

Silently, in recognition of the fact that this was the first morning after the death of Narenderji, they softly pottered about brushing teeth, making tea. When Satya started to make the bed, Sheila smiled, 'Leave it, don't worry, the maid will be here soon.'

'What luxury,' said Satya, realizing with a start that for once, she had no rancour in her heart as she said it, no bitterness. Only real pleasure that her friend had this and she could enjoy it this morning.

She was showering in the guest bedroom when the bell rang and Sheila let the cook in. By the time she came out, Satya could smell browning toast. Oh dear, should they be cooking?

'I think it's all right,' said Sheila, 'look, I'm not one for all these formalities, why trouble the whole world just for toast and tea? Ok, today we will just have a simple breakfast, why should it bother anyone else?'

So they sat down and had their breakfast, served sweetly by the caring cook. They made their way back to bed, Sheila leading Satya; as they got to the bedroom, they saw the bridal clothes still lying strewn around.

'Oh, I'm so sorry,' began Satya, embarrassed that she had not thought of picking them up last night.

'Oh, I'm so sorry,' began Sheila, embarrassed by the memory of what had happened last night.

Then they both laughed out loud. Satya put her hand over her mouth immediately, stopping her laughter. It wasn't right to laugh, not yet.

But Sheila pulled her hand off her mouth, 'It's all right, it's all right to laugh. Naren would not have minded. And he would be grateful and happy you were here with me today. Last night. I must have looked quite a sight. I must have given you a terrible fright, all dressed up!'

In spite of herself, Satya started laughing, 'Oh dear, I'm so sorry, but yes, it was such a shock to see you, like that ....'

They broke into peals of laughter as they leaned on each other's shoulders.

Somewhere their laughter turned into tears. They held onto each other, supporting each other, until they could bear to let the other go.

Then they started picking up the strewn clothes, the bangles, the kaleeras, the chura. They knew it was best to have it all put away before the maid came in. Finally, the velvet cover of the trunk was back in place. Satya turned to her friend. 'You know,' she said, putting her hands on her shoulders, 'you did look lovely, even now, even yesterday. You looked so sweet, so beautiful.'

9

A week passed. There was food every day from Kunti's or Tosh's house. After that first night every meal was taken care of. The chautha took place in the park in front of the house. It was a quiet affair, a granthi from the local gurudwara sang beautifully. A good photograph had been enlarged – a lovely smiling picture of Naren with his daughter, from which she had been cut away for the occasion. Rajnigandha fragranced the air, along with jasmine incense – his favourite. The rites done, the ashes immersed, the photograph garlanded on the wall. And it was done.

Satya asked Sheila if she wanted her to stay a little while longer. And Sheila immediately requested her to do so. It was good to have company, good to have a voice, footsteps stirring the air of the otherwise too quiet house. Satya turned out to be a remarkably soothing presence. It was comforting to have her help in the most painful part of the process. Annu and Sheila began to sort out clothes, papers, things, with help from Satya. The things left behind by a diligent man who squirreled away every paper, every scrap, every receipt for they may be of use some day or any contingency. There were some things Sheila wanted to hold on to, just for the memory. Annu was more firm about things she felt were clutter, but Satya could understand some memories were precious and should be held sacred, not consigned to the dustbin of time. She gave all the time to Sheila, not rushing her, listening to the story attached to each little scrap of their lives together. Like the story about the bus ticket. Where they'd gone and why. There was an interesting story linked to a restaurant bill. Sheila and Naren were celebrating their wedding anniversary combined with the celebration of Annu's graduation from medical college in Vellore.

Annu herself was spending some time with her friends, doing a Bharat Darshan. So they decided to splurge and go out for a nice dinner. The right hand side of the menu turned out to be rather steeper than they anticipated and they seriously considered leaving without ordering, but embarrassment coupled with a sense of fun made them stay on and order rather carefully. However, the bill came out substantially less than they expected and they were pleasantly surprised, it was well within their budget. That is, until they re-checked the bill just before leaving and found that they had not been billed for one of the dishes. Now here was a dilemma. Should they bring it to their waiter's notice and pay more than they had budgeted for? Or should they just leave quietly? Naren checked his wallet. He did not have enough cash to pay the amount it should have been. They could use the credit card Annu had got for them, but they were both conscientious objectors to plastic money. Eventually, grinning at each other like naughty children, they quickly left the restaurant knowing that they'd never go back there again!

But a few days later, they both confessed to each other they were burdened with guilt and would rather go back to the hotel and pay the balance amount. And they did. The restaurant manager was so pleased that he gave them free desserts right there and then and invited them to come back whenever they wanted. In fact, they made friends with the manager of the hotel, but it was he who came over to their house for ghar ka khana more often than they went over. That restaurant bill was saved, and now, both friends took turns to iron out the creases. It was yet another one of life's memories too precious to throw away.

Each little scrap had a piece of life attached to it. Finally, when Annu was getting more than a little impatient with the whole process, Sheila persuaded her to go back to work, or go home, assuring her Satya would help her.

It was a surprisingly pleasant time for Satya. She went back home only once, to collect some clothes and to tell the milkman she would not need milk for a few days. She told her neighbour Gopalji that he could take her newspaper. He was glad for he did not subscribe to one himself, but often borrowed hers to check on movie listings or obituaries. 'Why buy newspapers?' he often asked her. After all, they could get all the news they wanted much quicker on the television. The only time Gopalji wished he got the paper was when Satya called in the kabbadiwala and sold the paper, or when he borrowed it from her to wrap up something if he needed to.

So Satya and Sheila began to enjoy a peacefully happy time together. They still slept in the same room, giggling into the night over television programmes, watching the kind of shows they never would have if they had been alone – like Wife Swap and American Idol. They used separate bathrooms, though, and Satya truly enjoyed the nicely done up bathroom, rather than her MIG flat one where the taps often ran dry or leaked and the whole bathroom was completely soaked after a bath or when clothes were washed there. What a blessing these shower stalls were. And there were the additional safety guards – like railings – to hold on to when getting in or out of the bathing area, non-slip mats and a wonderfully high potty seat that did not strain the knees. 'All Annu's doing,' said Sheila proudly.

'You are blessed to have her,' said Satya and they both noted that again there was not a trace of bitterness or regret in her voice, only genuine happiness for her friend, on having such a lovely daughter. There had been a change in Sheila's life, that was obvious, but there had been an intrinsic change in Satya's life too. A soft happiness had gentled her, given her a glow, almost.

They decided – the two of them – they should resume their rummy mornings. It had been a week. 'Our friends are coming over, why not try to get back to our normal life – I don't know about the others, but I'm really missing the game, the get together. After all, for me its been an even longer time since I played, having been out of circulation because of all this,' said Sheila and Satya could see no real reason to disagree, except perhaps the propriety of it all. 'Oh who cares about propriety-shopriety, I mean, I know that Annu is all right with it. I've asked her and it is only what Naren would have wanted for me. He always said he did not want me to go on mourning him forever. What do you think?'

'If it's what you want ...,' began Satya diffidently, but then she brightened up. 'Yes, yes let's, what's the harm? If you want to and your daughter is ok with it and if it's what your husband – god rest his soul – would have wanted, then, yes, let's. Shall I call the others?'

Kunti and Tosh were surprised to get the call. More surprised to be invited over by Satya on Sheila's behalf. That too, for a party, a card party.

Tosh wondered whether to call Kunti and ask her what she thought, but the phone line was busy, as always, with one of the children. She really must get her own landline soon. She was always forgetting to charge her cell phone. She meant to try again later, but never did get around to it. Then, of course, she thought it best if she kept her feelings to herself. It was none of her business, if they had not consulted her, that was fine. After all, it was Sheila's decision. Or was it? 'I hope it isn't Satya pushing Sheila into something she's not quite ready for ...,' she thought, as she stood in front of her cupboard, wondering what she should wear. It should be something quietly appropriate. It was a party, but it was also in a house of mourning. Eventually, she chose a pale, pearly pink sari, pearls and a light lipstick with the slightest hint of shimmer. She wrapped herself in an off-white, fluffy Pashmina shawl. She smiled at herself in the mirror. Yes, she thought, she looked quite nice. When she got there, Kunti had already arrived, dressed in a grey silk salwar kameez that off-set the silver of her hair perfectly. Both of them looked at each other, approving the other's choice of attire. And then Kunti turned pointedly towards the 'hostesses' for that's what they were. Both of them. Tosh's perfectly plucked eyebrows rose a little in surprise that could not be hidden quickly enough. For before her stood Satya dressed in a wooly suit of red and green checks. But more than just the clothes, it was Satya herself, all aglow and carefree, almost. Not what she'd expected, not what they'd come to know of the stooped and wrinkled Satya, always with worry lining her forehead. She seemed to be years younger than they'd seen her ever before. And then there was Sheila. Another surprise. She was dressed in an elegant lime green sari, looking positively dazzling, again younger and glowing, radiant, almost. The house was looking spruced up, they had been used to seeing it dark and dingy, clean but cold. Now it was lit up with sunlight and flowers!

'How lovely everything looks,' cooed Tosh, collecting herself, camouflaging her surprise.

'Yes,' echoed Kunti, still in a bit of shock.

'Come, come in, please,' said Satya. Tosh and Kunti exchanged a look, how come Satya was being such a hostess here, even more so than in her own house! The card table was laid out. The counters stacked in neat piles, new cards crisp on the waiting table, made for a very welcoming sight. All, perfect, in fact, except for the fact that there had been a death here, in this very room just a week ago. But they were asked for tea, nimbu pani or coffee, as though all was perfectly normal. They placed their orders and Satya immediately started for the kitchen. 'Satya, sit,' said Sheila and they both burst into peals of laughter. Satya had tears rolling down her cheeks before she could gasp out, 'Oh dear, a whole week of this luxury of servants, and I still haven't got used to it. I'm afraid I'll never learn.'

'I tell you,' continued Sheila, 'every time something has to be done, or fetched, up she jumps like a real jack in the box. Sometimes I feel she should be leashed to keep her in her seat.' This brought fresh peals of laughter at the thought. Both Kunti and Tosh joined in half heartedly, it was as though they were suddenly strangers, or spectators in a play in which they had no part. Sheila noticed their discomfiture and immediately sobered up.

'Tosh behenji, Kunti, I hope it's all right with you?'

'What's all right?' started Kunti, although they all knew what she was talking about.

'Well, you know, meeting here, having our card party ... it's not too awkward for you, is it?'

Kunti laughed a high, false laugh, 'Oh ho, why should it be awkward, na? If you feel up to it, then why should any of us have objections, kyun Satya?'

Satya smiled and said, 'Bilkul, absolutely. I really don't think there is any need for awkwardness. All I know is that Sheila has been the best wife that anyone could possibly have been. She did all she could to make Narenderji comfortable. Now that he is no more, well, I think that she must get on with her life, don't you?'

'Hm.'

Sheila noticed their disapproval and said, 'If you think that it is not all right for you, if you're feeling uncomfortable, then we can ....'

'No, no, no, no ...,' they both cried. 'Of course not, Sheila, arrey, it is your comfort, your feelings, not ours that must be taken into account.'

Satya was about to say something, but she felt Sheila's hand quietly tap her knee, requesting that nothing more be said.

'Good, then,' she said brightly, and the game started. Kunti won the first hand, which lightened her mood a little, after that it was Satya all the way. She usually did not win much and was always a bit moody when having to pay up, even though the amount would be small. But today, she was winning hand after hand and her mood was zooming skywards.

'Oh, Sheila, you've been so lucky for me, just look, even in cards. Just look, I've got a thirteen card pure sequence. That's rare good luck.'

After a few more rounds, Satya giggled like a little girl, her cheeks flushed, her hands almost shaking with glee, 'Chalo, Sheila, now I'm going to get the khana peena; girls, there's a surprise for you!' She grinned at Sheila who almost winked back.

'Oh ho, now Satya, where is that leash that Sheila promised?' Tosh tried to join into the secret vibe between the two.

'No, no, Tosh, this time even I'm going to get up, our surprise is special, we've had so much fun doing it, that I'm not going to let the servants take all the credit.' The two disappeared into the kitchen.

Tosh and Kunti looked at each other. 'They seem happy, don't they?' began Kunti.

'Yes, but you know ....'

'Yes, it's too soon, isn't it? I must say, I'm not very comfortable.'

'And what's got into Satya, all of a sudden?'

'Really, I'm very glad to see her so happy, but at a time like this?'

'I know, but shh ... here they come ....' Both the women smiled extra brightly as the others returned from the kitchen. They were wheeling a trolley laden with food and plates and the fancy tea set, taken out of the cabinet for the first time since they'd been here.

'I just decided to use all the good stuff. Look, our wedding tea set, isn't it gorgeous?' The little pink rosebuds and gold edged curlicue cups were indeed very pretty. They'd been cleaned to a sparkle. A shadow work napkin covered a plate of what seemed to be little sandwiches and a tall, two-tiered cake platter held small tea-cakes all iced in pink, each dotted with a coloured Gems, the kind they'd done at children's birthday parties all those many years ago.

'Look,' cooed Sheila, 'we made them all ourselves!'

'Did you?' Kunti and Tosh said together, it was hard to believe. Sheila always had her cook make things and Satya got stuff from the market. In fact, Kunti and Tosh were the ones who occasionally made things for their parties. This was a first, and what an effort!

'Even the cakes? Which of you has been the secret cook all this time, never letting on to us, all these years?'

Satya and Sheila, still giggling like schoolgirls, confessed that the idea for doing this entire party had come out of a television programme.

'You know, one of those cookery shows.'

'Oof, but they're always so difficult, using all obscure ingredients.'

'Yes, mostly, but there's this one woman we've discovered over the last few days. She makes these absolutely easy recipes, full of yummy things, and all made in next to no time. Arrey, what's her name, Satya? You're the one that's so good at names.'

'Naturally, I can't help it, I've been a teacher all my life. Every year I had to learn ninety new names!'

'What's her name, then? Our new guru?'

'Nigella. There's this programme called Nigella Express on Discovery Travel and Living. She's just too good.'

'She was doing this children's birthday party special and we quickly got some paper and pencil.'

'Luckily you were in Sheila's house! In mine, by the time I'd found any paper and pencil, the programme would be over – the children you know, always removing things from where they should be kept,' said Kunti, trying to keep a foot in the conversation.

'Arrey, in Sheila's house there are all kinds of efficient things, all in the right place!'

And here Kunti and Tosh were regaled by their two friends as Sheila and Satya proceeded to demonstrate how the TV programme had gone. Accent and all, they mimed the making of the little cakes, the icing and with a big VOILA! They presented the platter to Kunti. She took one and bit into it. It was delicious, perfect. Tosh was impressed enough to take another although she was always careful about not eating too many sweets, being on one of her perpetual diets. Pleased with their success, Satya pushed on. 'And not as though with all that slaving in the kitchen, this Nigella has a flat chest, no ji, you should see her ....'

She glanced around for something to use as props and her eyes lighted on two wicker baskets that were kept for the cards and counters. Quickly, without her usual school-marmishness, she stuffed them up into her kameez from underneath and up onto her chest. 'Whoooo!' she laughed, 'You've got to see them!' she laughed, patting her newly enlarged breasts.

Sheila guffawed and sat down on her seat. But Kunti pushed her seat back and was now standing up, in a towering rage.

'Enough!' she commanded, 'both of you, just, just stop it now, enough, bas, bahut ho gaya!'

Stunned, they looked at her: Satya still had the baskets inside her kameez.

'Kunti ... please ...,' pleaded Tosh, she hated an unpleasant scene, although she could understand Kunti's displeasure.

'Oh ho, don't take it to heart, bhai, it's just a joke, just a harmless joke, na?' Sheila tried to soothe Kunti, but the latter was unstoppable now. She found the way these two so-called friends of hers were behaving right in the middle of the mourning period to be inappropriate and downright abhorrent. Also, if the truth be told, she was more than a little, what – jealous? Hurt? That Satya had become such a comrade, leaving her so much out in the cold.

'No, no Sheila, I think this has gone on far enough! You, you, well, you must be in shock over your loss, so you're not behaving rationally, not ... properly. But you? You, Satya? I would have thought that you, being a teacher would have known that this, this whole p-p-party, with all this celebration ... this ... this ...,' she splayed her hands out in disgust, as though she'd been confronted with some filth. 'I would have thought you'd have the sense to guide our friend better. If I'd only known what you were up to, why, I would have come and stayed here myself. No matter what – I would have been here to see she was not being misguided! Hai hai, what will the neighbours say? Does Annu know of all this ... this ...?' Again, she waved her hands at the vulgarity of it all and then sat back with a thud onto her chair, dropping her head into her hands, as though unable to take in anymore of this scene.

There was a stunned silence. No one knew what to say or do. They'd had their differences before, but never had there been such an open confrontation.

Sheila remained seated, her eyes glassed over by tears that were too frightened to fall. She had really thought, no – believed, that they would understand. In fact she'd expected that they would be happy and pleased that she had recovered so well from her loss, had been able to get on with her life so well. But instead, here was condemnation of her behaviour, her actions. In fact, she was suddenly consumed with self-doubt. Was she so much in shock that she'd behaved in such a horribly indecent manner? Or worse, was she not in shock at all? Was she just relieved that her invalid husband was gone and she was 'celebrating' his passing? A shudder of horror shook her at this possibility. She had no words to say. But she let her tears fall now.

Satya looked at Sheila, thinking that she would say something, explain. It was really for her to do that. But when she looked at the tears pooling into Sheila's palms resting in her lap, her shock turned to anger. For once, she thought, for once I'm going to speak my mind.

'Who are you to criticize her? Who are you to sit in judgement over her actions? Or mine, for that matter?'

Kunti stood up straight, almost nose to nose with Satya, but Satya was taller, and so Kunti was forced to look up.

'I am a person who has Sheila's best interests at heart and yours too,' Kunti asserted.

'And who are you to know anybody else's best interest?' Satya snapped, not backing down as always. 'Why do you feel that what you decide for us is the right thing and that what we decide is the wrong thing?'

'Well, I don't think that anyone in their right minds would believe that this party, this celebration, is the right thing in the circumstances. Tosh? Don't you think that this is wrong? Tosh? Why don't you say something?'

Tosh hated controversy; she would do anything for peace. What should she do now, whose side should she take? 'Well, of course this is all, rather, well, unusual, no doubt, but you know, as Satya says, who are we to judge? If both of them felt, you know … it's ok, then, why should we have objections?'

She hoped that she had placated both sides. But Kunti's stand did not soften. She saw Satya place a protective hand on Sheila; there was a new closeness between them.

'I don't see the need to justify anything, to you or to anyone else, but I … all I want to say is this … Sheila has had a hard life for the past few years. She has looked after her husband beautifully. She did the best she could to make him as comfortable as possible. She put her own life on hold, just to be with him, to care for him. How many times, how many weeks, she didn't even come out of the house. Because that's what he needed, that's what she did. Now that he is gone, there is no need for her to continue suffering. I don't see the need for a prolonged mourning period when it has been a relief for poor Narender bhai sahib to have passed on. I don't think that Sheila needs to worry about what others think. Except maybe her daughter – who supports her mother getting back to living her life. She has proved herself more than adequately. Now let her enjoy her time, her self, her life. And we, who are her friends, should at least understand this and support her. Help her return to normal life, not stand in judgement over what is proper and what is not. And I don't see why we should worry about what the neighbours will say. Bhad mein jaye this dakiya noosi thinking. I don't care for tradition and conservative thinking just for the sake of it!'

Sheila was crying softly. By now, Satya had both her hands on her friend's shoulders; sometimes one hand was stroking Sheila's head, lovingly.

'I'm sorry,' it was Sheila who spoke before anyone else could. The servants were hovering in the background, surprised by the raised voices. They themselves had had misgivings about the whole party and gaiety, but of course, it was not their place to express any opinion.

'I'm so sorry, you are right, it is not proper. We … I … should not have done this. It is too soon …,' she sobbed.

Tosh put her hand out and covered Sheila's shoulder and Satya's hand. 'No,' she said gently, 'no, you are absolutely right, Satya, it … this is right, as it should be. I, for one, am happy to see you happy.'

Kunti shifted a bit uncomfortably, she was alone in her corner now, but she could see the sense in what they were saying. It's just that she had not thought about it at all. She'd been brought up assuming that recent widows must behave in a certain, set way, never thinking that there could be another way that could also be right.

'I – I'm happy too. I know that you have done so much. You don't need to do anything for show. I'm glad to see you've done so well, after such a difficult time,' Kunti said, looking at Sheila. She couldn't bring herself to look at Satya. She was embarrassed by her outburst. From the corner of her eye she saw Satya slipping the baskets out of her shirt and putting them back on the table. Satya thought, 'Yes, perhaps that joke was a tad out of place, at this point in time.'

'So now, do you mind if I have another of your delicious pastries?' Kunti laughed a little too loudly, forcing mirth to cover her embarrassment.

'It would be our pleasure,' said Satya sweetly, just slightly emphasizing the 'our' to tell them that the two of them were a team.

'Be careful of your sugar, Kunti,' but Tosh's warning was delivered with a smile.

The rest of the afternoon passed peacefully. The gaiety, of course, came down a few notches, but each of them worked hard to cover the earlier unpleasantness with small talk and tinkling laughter. Smooth and shining like the iced pastries. Satya's winning streak seemed to be over, but triumph edged the straightness of her back. She had won at more than cards today.

As they left, Kunti hugged Sheila and then Satya; she whispered into Satya's ear, 'I'm glad you did this, I'm glad you are here for Sheila, thank you.'

10

One week turned into two and then three. Although she was so comfortable being here and Sheila was obviously relaxed and happy, it was a comment from the maid that made Satya decide it was time to go home. Maybe she didn't really mean it the way it came out, but Munni's comment – 'It's so good that you could stay soooo long with madamji, Satya memsahib. It is lucky you didn't have to rush back for anyone in your own house' – cut Satya to the quick. Not least because it was the bare truth. But if this was how the servants felt, and maybe they discussed it amongst themselves, then it was time to go. It was the only self-respecting thing to do and Satya was nothing if not particular about her self-respect.

Sadly, without saying anything to Sheila as yet, Satya went to the guest room – *her room.* Initially, she'd just brought one little overnighter. Since then, she'd been getting more of her clothes and things in plastic shopping bags. Oh dear, how was she to pack everything up neatly now and not leave here looking like a bag lady? She decided to be packed and ready to leave before telling Sheila about it. But now, clearly, she was going to need to borrow a small suitcase from her. It was then that it struck Satya. She had really never planned on leaving at all! Somewhere subconsciously, she'd been bringing it all here in bits and pieces, never thinking about how she would take it all away, because maybe, just maybe, she'd thought she'd never need to.

Satya almost recoiled from the thought in horror. What presumption! What thoughtless assumption! The lack of self-respect it implied. How could she have brought this on herself?

No, she decided firmly, no, she wasn't going to ask for anything more. She'd come as a giver of comfort and succour in her friend's hour of need. But then she'd turned into a taker, partaking of her richer friend's comforts and facilities. She stood in front of the bathroom mirror now.

'Potty!' she said to the sallow yellow face that stared back at her, 'Potty, potty, chichi yellow,' she accused the face. 'You're a shit, shitty yellow. Flush yourself away.' Her tears welled as the familiar self-loathing rose. From her toes, flooding every fiber of her being; from fingernails to her head.

'Shitty, kutti, bitch!' her fingernails were digging into the softness of her thin-skinned wrists. Bands of pure pain wound themselves around her head, tightening, like a vise.

'Ah!' the slap across her face was stinging, startling her as though the hand had been someone else's. She pulled at her hair, trying to tear open the bands of pain. But the pain only worsened. She was dizzy with it and the nausea rose with the bile, turning her throat, her mouth, to acid. When she finally threw up neatly and expertly into the pot, so no one would know, the vomit was green and burned her on its way out. She clutched at the coolness of the plush flush tank, until she felt steady enough to leave the solidness of it and make her way to the sink where she splashed cool water onto her face and neck. There was shame, but also relief. She'd thrown out more than physical bile. She looked at her wrists. Oh dear, she'd have to pull out something long-sleeved to wear. She couldn't let poor dear Sheila see the scratch marks and blood on her wrists. The fresh ones from just now as well as some from before. Sheila must not know. No one must get to know.

She stuffed her pathetic little belongings into pathetic little plastic bags. She was done and ready to go. To flee now. She looked around the room. Her room. Please, please let me say *my* room. On a sudden impulse she went to the bed, tried to kneel as in prayer, as they were taught in school. But she was suddenly afraid if she did that, she wouldn't be able to get up off the floor. So she sat, or rather sank onto the edge of the bed: not quite sure what to do, but feeling the need to do something that would mark her determination to leave. She folded her hands and bent her head.

'Dear God ... dear, dear God ....' But 'thank you' was what came to her mind. 'Thank you God for the time I've spent here.' Yes, she was grateful for what she had received. She was grateful, too she had realized she needed to leave before being told to outright by her friend. She patted the firmness of the bed, but as she was about to stand, she bent instead and lay her head for a fleeting, precious moment on the pillow. 'Thank you,' she said to it, 'thank you for the sweetest sleep I've ever, ever had.' Although she'd spent her nights in Sheila's room, afternoons naps had been here. Then she turned her face, burying it into the pillow and kissed it. Soft, at first. But then her kiss became harder, more passionate. She pulled the pillow out from under the bedcover, cradling it in her arms. Then she slipped her hand under the pillow slip, kissing, caressing, loving it urgently.

Like a man.

Finally, she managed to pull herself away, embarrassed by the intimacy. But she didn't feel foolish; instead she felt replete. Satisfied. Calmer now, she straightened the bed after stripping it of its sheets and the pillow case. She put these into the bucket for a wash. With one final glance at the mirror, armed with a smile of satisfaction that the yellow of her personality was more sunny and clean now, she stepped out of the room.

'Kya Satya, I was wondering where you'd gone. Look what I've found!' There was a Scrabble board all set up and ready to play.

'Sheila,' Satya sat down across from her friend, on what had now become *her* chair. 'Sheila behen, I've been thinking ....'

'Oh ho, all this thinking-winking is no good, never does anyone any good, I feel.' Then she looked closely at Satya's face, all serious, and with a start of misgiving she asked, 'Par hua kya? Is something the matter?'

'Sheila, I've had such a very wonderful time here.'

'Yes, Satya, so have I. Par why do I sense a "but" here?'

'Nahin, not that, it's just, you know ....' Now that the moment was at hand, she did not know how to say it. 'Well ... my dear sister, I just, you know ...'

'What Satya? Just say it, you're starting to worry me now, come now, spit it out. You know I hate suspense.'

'Well, I just think it's time I went back home now, you know?'

Sheila seemed to visibly deflate before Satya's eyes. There was silence, just silence as Sheila looked down at her hands, and alternately shook and nodded her head as though in a silent conversation with herself. Satya waited, not knowing what else to do, but finally, when Sheila wouldn't say anything, she burst out, 'Sheila, say something, na? What are you thinking? Now you're the one who's scaring me.'

'Yes, home,' Sheila whispered, nodding again. 'Home, yes. Home.'

'Yes, Sheila, I should be going home na? It was never supposed to be forever.'

But Sheila didn't seem to have heard as she continued softly, as though rebuking herself. 'Home, yes. It was foolish, stupid of me to think, to hope, that you could make this your home. That you would think that you *were* home. I mean really, really your home.' She looked up and smiled.

To Satya's horror, tears welled up in Sheila's eyes and splashed onto her spectacles, blurring her beautiful eyes. Then, in a gush of emotion and words, she sobbed, 'It was so wrong of me to have kept you from your home for so so long. To have expected you to give up your life, just for me. To have thought that you would feel at home. To think that you were completely happy ....'

'Happy? Of course, of course I'm happy. I couldn't have been any happier. I haven't been any happier, ever. Ever!' Satya rushed over to Sheila's side and held her hands, trying to stem the tide of tears.

'Yes, I know you've been happy, but not as happy as I am, was .... I'd imagined that this was going to be for the rest of my, our, lives.' Sheila was howling like a baby now. 'I thought you *were* home, I thought you *were*!' She bawled; her eyes and nose were running. Her glasses were off now and she was completely blinded as much by the lack of them as by her overwhelming sorrow.

Her maid came running in, wondering what could have happened and found her memsahib wailing away. 'Kya hua, par hua kya?' She rushed over to her, kneeling at her feet and looking accusingly at poor Satya who was looking guilty. What could she have done, wondered the maid, after all her Sheila memsahib had done for her, is this how she was repaying her kindness? Making her cry?

'Tell her, tell her, na,' Sheila appealed to the maid, 'tell her not to go!'

'What? Where is she going, where are you going?' the bewildered maid asked Satya.

'No, I was just saying that I should go home now. After all, I'd come just for a day or two and I've stayed so long, so I just thought ....' But this pronouncement brought a fresh flood of tears as Sheila grabbed them both by their hands, 'Tell her, please tell her not to go. I want her here. Please.' Then she buried her head into the maid's shoulder and confessed through more tears, 'I don't want to be alone. I want her here.'

With a guilty start everything fell into place for the maid. She and the cleaning woman had plotted to talk to Satya memsahib and drop a hint that it was time she left and went to her own house. They'd been talking amongst themselves and thought that their own memsahib would never be able to tell her to go and they'd thought that this would be the best way. But their plan had worked too well. In fact it had backfired.

Still kneeling on the floor, Munni put her hand on Satya memsahib's knees. She hoped that she would not tell Sheila about their conversation. With a desperate appeal in her eyes, she pleaded, 'Arrey Satya memsahib, why should you go? What is the need? We love to have you here. It is so nice to see you and Sheila memsahib together, don't go, please don't go.'

'See?' said Sheila looking up, her tears stemming finally, but her nose still running, 'See? I don't want you to go, they don't want you to go. Please stay Satya, please stay, at least a little while longer.'

'I just, I thought ...,' but Satya had no words, she was overwhelmed with the feeling of being wanted, needed desperately. She'd never felt that before. 'Oh dear, I thought – I thought I'd overstayed my welcome ....'

'NO!' cried the maid and Sheila together, 'No! You are most welcome.'

'Oh please, please stay. Stay a little longer!'

11

More and more things made their way from Satya's home into Sheila's. Although she was very happy here, Satya was also conscious of the fact that she did not want to appear like the poor friend sponging off the more affluent one. But both Sheila and, even more so, Annu begged her to stay a while longer, if it was not an inconvenience. It certainly wasn't one. Satya had nothing really to go back to. She made a twice weekly visit back, just to make sure things were well and to get the house cleaned. The more things were layered in dust, the more she felt like just leaving it once and for all. Not that she would tell anyone that, just a thought that crept into her mind. One that had never struck her all this time. But now that there was an alternative home to go to, this one seemed tedious. Climbing up all those steps especially made her tired. More tired than she had ever felt before. She was always glad to be back at Sheila's, bathing in a lovely bathroom, with plenty of hot water and a shower that you could turn to gentle or jet, or massage.

To make up for the fact she was a guest, she started doing some of the cooking. It had been years since she'd actually taken an interest in cooking, but she had been well taught by her mother and grandmother. It was reassuring to see how easily it was all coming back to her. She felt at home in the kitchen now, rolling out crisp matthies, peanut butter cookies, jams and achars, casseroles and baked vegetables. The regular, everyday cooking was done by the cook, but at least once a day, Satya would produce a special something, making sure each time, to put aside something for the maids as well, so that they would not feel as though she had usurped their domain. She was particular about buying ingredients for the things she cooked herself. At first Sheila objected. 'There's no need, Satya, all the grocery comes home, why you need to go out and spend your money and pay for all this?' But after a while, she let it go. If it made Satya feel more comfortable and more at home, then it was all right. They often ate the special treats in front of the television, watching more cooking programmes, or sometimes a rented movie.

But even more than the cooking, it was Satya's help with all the paperwork that was appreciated by both Sheila and her daughter. Satya, who had always managed all the umpteen files, folders, papers and bills even for her own parents, was adept at it. She went out and bought some multi-pocketed files. Slowly, she separated the house and property papers from the investment papers, put aside passports, election cards and PAN cards. There were many useless, expired papers and empty cheque books over ten years old. These she put into a separate folder that was to stay at the bottom of all the papers. The insurance claims had to be filed. This was painful for Sheila, so Satya handled most of it. But only after many reassurances from everyone that no one thought that she was prying into private, family affairs.

One evening, there was a knock on the door. A fat Sikh gentleman with a heavily waxed beard and mustache stood there. The maid took his card to the two women as they were playing a quiet game of rummy between themselves.

Inderjit Singh
Estate and Property
For all your needs for
Buy/Sell
Flat, Kothi, Farm, Office

With his telephone number under the descriptor, 'tring tring'. And there were two mobile numbers, of course.

'What does he want with us?'

'Forget it, just send him away.'

The maid took the card back to the door, but returned saying the gentleman wanted to meet the lady of the house for just five minutes. He said he had something very urgent to say. Reluctantly curious, they invited him into the living room. It wasn't often that they met strangers, especially gentlemen.

He waddled in, hands folded, ubiquitous, 'Satsriakal madamjis,' he said, looking from one to the other, obviously wondering which of the two he should be focusing on.

'Satsriakal,' they both replied together. They realized immediately that he was trying to make out who was who, but they weren't going to make it any easier for him, at least until they figured out what he wanted.

'So sorry to hear about your late husbandji,' he said, turning first to Satya and then to Sheila. They were sitting on opposite ends of the coffee table, so he actually had to turn his whole body, since he had no neck to speak of. It was certainly awkward for him, and they were perversely enjoying his discomfiture. Both of them had taken an instant, instinctive dislike to him. There was something smarmy about the man. They both just nodded, acknowledging his condolence. Now he was really confused. He tried again, 'Er – Mrs Narender Singhji, are you ...?' he asked Satya. She neither denied nor agreed.

'What is it you want?' was all she said.

'O ji, I am very sorry to hear about your late husband.'

'You knew him?' This time he had to turn himself, chest upward to face Sheila.

'No, no, ji, I did not have the pleayures of knowing the great man.'

'Ah, hmm ...?'

He looked down at his fat hairy hands, wishing they would just tell him which one was the widow, and then he could do this better.

'Mr Inderjit Singh, please tell us what you want: you said you'd just take five minutes.' This time he swiveled towards Satya, beginning to get faintly suspicious that they were doing this purposely to confuse him. All right, they were obviously close; he'd just go ahead and talk to the taller one. She seemed to be more in command. They must be sisters, he concluded. Could not be anything else.

'Madamji,' he began his well-rehearsed spiel, 'Madamji, I know that this is a hard time for you ....' He glanced at Satya for some reaction; getting none, he stole a glance at the other, but both mirrored the same expression, so he pressed on. 'If there is anything, anything at all that I can do at my end to ease your suffering, you only have to ask, behenji, you are like a sister to me, elder sister.'

He waited. Then, when neither said anything, he continued, moving in for the kill as it were, 'Madamji, I know that now a house like this, an old house that is, so big, may become difficult for you to manage, now with dear uncleji gone … so, if there is anything at all, that I can do to help ….'

'Help, how, exactly?'

'No, no, you don't have to think now or in a hurry. No hurry, madam, no hurry at all. My card is with you, whenever you feel like giving a tinkle; please feel free to call upon me as a brother.'

'Why would we want to call you? Why don't you just come out and say what you have come to say. Then be on your way.' Satya's voice was sharp. So this tall thin one was definitely the lady of the house.

'You see, madamji, auntyji, in this day and age, your age, especially, such a big houses is difficult to run for single, or, or even double ladies, heh, heh. So many old peoples nowadays, they are selling off the big old houses and moving to much better flats, modern, easy to manage and with all amenities.'

'Are you suggesting that you will buy this house?'

'Eggjacktly!' He beamed now, finally they had got the point. So what were they, sisters? They didn't look like sisters, eggjacktly.

'But this house is not for sale.'

'No, no, of course not, it is your dear abode, your family property; only I am saying to put the idea in your mind. Anytime, anytime, please feel frees to call upon my services, should any such need arise, that is all. Thangs, many thangs ….' He lifted himself off the chair with difficulty, almost taking the chair with his backside, lifting it off the floor. With much bowing and scraping, he left them, congratulating himself. He was obviously the first to have contacted them. In this business, one had to move fast in order to succeed. Of course, they hadn't given it too much thought, or any thought at all, but the planting of the seed was the first step for a good harvest.

He hesitated as he was shown the door by the maid. Should he ask which of them was the widow and what was the relationship between the two? But no, he decided, it was enough for one day.

The two women looked at each other and smiled, 'Accha budhu banaya, kyun?'

'Yes, we made a right idiot of him, didn't we?'

'Poor fellow, I began to feel a bit sorry for him, he was so confused,' they laughed.

But there was the bigger question to think of as well.

'You know, it is a thought that has occurred to me ...,' Sheila said softly.

'Don't start worrying about it right now, Sheila, there will be enough time to address these things. Give yourself some time to rest your soul, get other things in order, phir, Annu and Sonjoy ke saath, you can talk about how and where you want to live.'

'You are right, but this old house really does demand a lot of hard work. I'm not sure I have the energy, or even the money for all the upkeep. As it is, there are so many things that I've just let go already.'

'Of course not, you run such a perfect house!'

'Ah, but look at the garden, I just don't have the himmat or stamina anymore to keep the garden the way I used to. I was so proud of it and Naren really loved to sit out there.'

'So, now you'll have some time, you can re-start it.'

'Hai, but for who? Sometimes I do think that it will be easier just to go to a smaller, modern flat where one doesn't have to think of hassles like electricity and water and all.'

'Well, there's time to think of all that, don't worry about it now. Come on, forget the fat Sardarji and let's get on with our game.'

But Sheila was rubbing her arthritic fingers and wishing she could really have a place to stay where the wiring didn't short-circuit and the pipes didn't leak and the weeds didn't reclaim the garden as though they were the masters there. She must remember to buy some Yog Raj Gugulu for the pain in her fingers.

Satya tried hard not to think of the house being sold or demolished. She loved this old house and loved her life in it.

12

A few days later, Tosh offered to host a card morning at her house. While it was initially agreed upon, Sheila suddenly came into Satya's room in tears.

'Arrey, Rani, what's happened? Arrey, arrey, don't cry, come, come,' she crooned and calmed Sheila down. 'Now tell me, what's happened to upset you so much?' She was talking to her as though she were a child, but it was the right tack to take, for Sheila sobbed in a childlike voice, 'I don't, I don't want to go …'

'Where? Where don't you want – to Tosh behenji's?' Sheila nodded, then looked up, still childlike. 'I don't know what's come over me, Satya, I just, I just don't feel up to going out, I … I want to be at home ….' She dissolved into fresh tears.

'There, there, of course you don't want to go out, it's only natural.'

'Is it?'

'Yes, of course, you've only just lost your beloved husband; of course you don't want to go out. It's all right, I'll call the others right now, just don't worry.'

As she made to leave, Sheila caught her hand. 'Satya, I don't know how to thank you enough, you've been such a blessing … what would I do without you?'

'Well, don't worry about that one; because you don't have to do without me, I'm here na?'

'Promise?'

'Promise!' with a smile, Satya reached for the phone and dialed Tosh's number.

'Wait, wait, oh don't!'

Quickly Satya disconnected. 'Kya hua?'

'Oh ho, they'll feel so bad. After last time, I don't want to upset them again.'

'Look, right now, the most important thing to do is what you want; just don't think about anyone else. And as for last time, they really did understand that it was wrong, what they were thinking. You know they did.'

'Yes ....'

'So, I'm going to call them. Then, whenever you're ready, we'll go out. If you feel like it, we can have them over here sometime instead, if that's better for you?'

'Yes, yes, oh yes, I'd like that, even today, even now, I'd really like it if they can come over instead, do you think they'll agree?'

'Let's ask, ok?'

Of course they did understand, 'that's what friends are for'. Tosh quickly packed the snacks she'd prepared and decided to leave them in the car and then see if Sheila was ok with her bringing them in. Kunti arrived with a bunch of white carnations and some asters from her garden.

Sheila hugged each of them warmly, thanking them for their understanding. They decided not to play cards that day. No one was quite up to it. Instead, after the snacks had been brought in from Tosh's car, they sat and chatted.

Sheila started off with praising Satya a lot for all the peace and efficiency that she'd brought into her life. Satya, in turn, said she'd never felt happier in her personal life, never felt so wanted.

'Needed, bhai, kya wanted, I need you!' laughed Sheila.

'Well then, the need is on both sides. You don't know what a pleasure it's been to wake up in the morning to find someone in the bed next to me.'

'Even if it's not a man?'

They giggled as Satya continued, 'Well, I wouldn't know, would I? I've never woken up next to a man. All I know is, I love not having to wake up in an empty room, to an empty life.'

They all knew what that was like. Tosh's home was also empty now, although it had been full of life at one time, whereas Satya's had always been that way.

'Oh dear, I don't know what its going to be like going home to an empty nest again.'

'Then don't.'

Sheila's statement was greeted with sudden silence. They all held their breath.

'What ...?' Satya's voice was tremulous, her smile tried not to be too eager. Had she heard right, had she understood correctly? Did Sheila really mean ... forever ...?

Tosh and Kunti too, held their breaths; this was something neither of them had ever thought of before. Was this a good idea?

Sheila nodded at Satya. 'Don't, don't go back. Where is the need? You're alone, now I'm alone. There's so much space here, we're happy together, aren't we?'

'Happier than I've ever been in all my life!'

'Then stay. Just give up your flat; put it on rent. You're unnecessarily spending money on your cleaning woman. You don't need to anymore. Just stay on with me.'

'Just like that?'

'If you'd like it, I'd love it,' said Sheila simply. Satya's hands floated up to her face and came to rest around her cheeks, cupping her mouth rounded to an O. She couldn't believe what had just happened. It was too good to be true. She looked at Tosh and Kunti, looking for approval. Tears sparkled in her eyes.

'You don't know how much this means to me. Just your asking. I don't know what to say.'

Tosh said, 'Then don't say anything, just think about it. There'll be things you'll need to sort out.'

'No, I don't need to think. I know, know for sure. I would like nothing more than to stay on here with you, Sheila. I've lived in that flat for thirty-six years and it's never felt like home. And here, I've just been here what – even less than a month and I already feel like this has been the best home I've ever lived in. And there's really not much I need to sort out, nothing that can't be done before the first of next month.'

Sheila stood up and took Satya in her arms. 'Welcome,' she said as they hugged each other tight.

It was a new beginning, a new bond. Kunti and Tosh exchanged a look: was there a touch of envy in it, a wish that they, too, would be included into this circle of friendship? Then Satya held up her hand, 'Wait, just one moment. It is a big decision, Sheila, I think that you should ask Annu, see if she's all right with this.'

'No, no, I know she will be more than happy that I have someone with me, especially a good friend with whom I get on so well.'

'Still, it's better to ask.'

'Arrey, I know her na, she will have no objections, and in any case, it's my decision to take, no?'

'All the same,' said Tosh, 'I think Satya is right, just speak to Annu about it, what's the harm?'

Then they told Tosh and Kunti about the slimy sardar, as they called him. 'It was too funny, he couldn't make out which of us was the owner of the house, and he couldn't even turn easily to face us.'

Satya did a great imitation of the man and had them in splits. 'He had this huge stomach – Kunti, don't worry, this time I'm not going to stuff any papayas into my kameez!'

They were practically rolling around on the floor laughing. The maids smiled too, it was good to see their memsahib so happy. But suddenly they noticed that Kunti's tears were not of laughter, or at least, not only of laughter, there were real tears rolling down her cheeks.

'Kunti, Kunti what has happened?'

'Why are you crying?'

'Has something happened at home?'

'Are you not well?'

'I'm as well as I can be!' sobbed Kunti, putting on her best drama queen act for all she was worth. 'As well as can be expected from a woman who has been abandoned by those who should be closest to her.'

Sheila was immediately by her side, mothering, quite happy to be playing her nurturing role again. It made her feel whole again. She poured another cup of elaichi tea, made her sip it, calmed her down and then they all sat around her to listen to her tale of woe.

"They're leaving me!' wailed Kunti, although her tears had dried by now. 'My sons are such chamchas of their wives, I tell you! Now they're leaving me.'

'They're shifting out of the house?'

'Have they got transferred out of town?'

'No, no, nothing like that, catch them leaving a house where they can live for free.'

'Oh no, are they sending you away somewhere?'

'Huh, they wouldn't dare do any such thing! Chuck me out of my house, oof, I'd kill them if they tried any such stunt.' Kunti was remarkably recovered from her tears, back into fighting mode.

So what then, they asked.

'They're all going off together on a holiday to Europe!' she announced triumphantly, looking around to receive their looks and words of horror and sympathy. But instead, she got blank stares.

'So?' began Tosh, voicing everyone's question.

'So? All of them, don't you see, both boys, their wives, their children, all going so far away, without the least concern for me, for the fact I'll be left all alone.'

'Arrey, Kunti, you know, you should be happy they can all take a holiday together …,' began Satya.

'Happy, why should I be happy?'

'Well, at least be happy your children, their wives, their children all get on so well they can take holidays together. That they want to. Look around you, so many sisters, brothers, they don't even talk to each other, so many wives don't let their husbands meet their families, so many children don't want to spend a minute with their cousins, let alone a whole foreign trip. You should be happy.'

'Theek hai, what you say may be right, but what about me? Don't you think they have an obligation to be with me?'

'They are with you all year round. Let them go off for a little while.'

'What all year round? They make me work like an ayah, worse, like a slave, then, when it's their holiday, they go off and leave me behind.'

'You'd like to go with them?'

She hesitated. The fact was, that they used to ask her to come along once upon a time, but because she always resisted going, they had stopped asking her. 'Well, they could ask, at least.'

'But you wouldn't go, would you?'

'Kya, these small, small hotels they stay in, who would want to? Bathrooms the size of matchboxes and that too, you have to share with others. And a cup of coffee for sixty rupees or more. And then you have to make your own beds and wash your own bartans. Na baba, who would want to leave the comforts of one's own home to go there, mara mari?'

'So then, let them go, na, how does it matter?'

'That's not the point.'

'Then what is?'

'When they need me, they just make full use of me, whether its baby sitting, or making something, or whatever, it's always assumed that I'm available.'

'You're lucky, you know, you're lucky someone wants you, needs you, you're lucky to have your grandchildren growing up next to you. Not far, far away,' said Tosh, thinking about her own children and grandchildren.

'But then, when they have to go, then they don't even ask me, not only if I want to go, but it's ok if they're gone. They don't even ask – that's my point. Am I wrong?'

Tosh shook her head, it seemed that she wanted to say something, but wouldn't let it out. Sheila patted her hand. 'It's all right, you know, just come out and say whatever's on your mind. You don't have to hide anything from us, you know that.'

'No, well, it's just, just ....'

They waited, knowing there was an internal struggle taking place in the normally placid and positive Tosh. It took her a near-physical effort to say something bad about someone, especially someone close. But she knew if she could really express herself anywhere, it was here, in the safe cocoon of this company.

'I know it's a wonderful opportunity for my children to take their children all around the world. Kabhi Moscow aur kabhi Mexico, but I do wish they'd sometimes make an effort to come here too, after all, I am alone. It would be nice to meet them all more often.'

'But you said that your grandchildren hate it when they're here, they fuss and fuss.'

'Yes, of course they did when they came here last, but if they were to come more often, then the children, too, would get used to it. If they never bring them, then they'll only be happy with five-star holidays. And as for my daughter, well, she can hardly ever find time for her own children. I just can't believe the life she and her husband lead, rushing to work early morning, coming back late at night. Their kitchen is more like a cemetery than the heart of the home. They all eat on the metro, or underground or whatever they have in America, so that they don't have to do dishes when they get home. But still, when they do take a holiday, I wish sometimes they'd think of India and Nani rather than some fancy foreign soil. Or if they are going, maybe, as Kunti says, they could consider asking me to join them, sometimes, at least. Tell me, am I wrong?'

Well, they agreed, she wasn't completely wrong. Neither Tosh nor Kunti was wrong. It was certainly nice to be asked. Each one talked about feeling let down by those who one should have been able to depend on.

'Don't we sound like a bunch of bitter biddies!' laughed Tosh who, for once, had relinquished her role of peacemaker and joined in the fray with her own personal feelings.

Finally Kunti said, 'I don't like being alone anymore. There was a time when I liked it. I'd be happy having the house to myself. But lately, I don't know, I can't sleep in an empty house.'

'Then join us here,' Sheila cried. 'That's the perfect solution. Let them go off on their holiday, and we'll have our own vacation right here. Kyun Satya, wouldn't that be fun?'

'That's a great solution, Kunti, we'll have a blast, as the kids say now.'
'Oh, I have an even better idea,' Satya was clapping her hands in delight. 'Tosh, you come too!' Then her hands flew to her mouth, embarrassed. 'Er ... that is, if it's all right with you, Sheila, sorry, I shouldn't be doing this in your house.'

'It's your house, Satya, as much as it's mine. I think it's a great idea. Tosh, you come too.'

'No, no, of course I couldn't.'

'Come on, you had quite a good time when you were over at Kunti's.'

'But that was for just one evening, this is for ....'

'Ok, so you come for the weekend, huh? Let's have a weekend for ourselves.'

They all clamoured for Tosh to join them, even Kunti who till this moment had not quite made up her mind.

And so it was decided, they were going to have a delicious weekend.

'Forget all about our dietary restrictions.'

'No getting up early for morning walks.'

'No eating light, early dinner.'

'No rules.'

'Yes,' they all shouted together, 'NO RULES!!'

The servants shook their heads in the kitchen, what's got into these memsahibs, they wondered.

Like schoolgirls, they giggled over their planning.

'Bhai, I want to have tandoori chicken.'

'Should we order khana from outside?'

'Not pizza, please, it gives me indigestion.'

'But I love pizza, I never eat it, but I do love it.'

'I swear, why have all these things come now, just when we don't have the stomachs to digest them?'

'Or the teeth to chew them?'

'I say, let our teeth and stomachs get used to it, this is what we're going to eat. We can have Isabgol afterwards so that we have no problems next morning!'

'Yes, yes, Isabgol can be our dessert.'

'Rubbish, I want Satya's cakes – will you make those little pink icing walas again?'

'Of course, why not?'

'No, no, none of us should go to the kitchen.'

'It's really no problem, I'll teach Mary how to do most of it, theek hai?'

'No, no, don't do that, then she'll run away and get a fancy job with some firangis, or something.'

'I tell you, you're so lucky to have Mary, how long have you had her?'

'Thirteen years or so now, I think.'

'Good help is so hard to find, you should see the kind of ayahs my daughter-in-law is bringing in. Every month a new one, so unsafe, what with all these murders and all. I say, Sheila, tell your Mary to help na?'

'Oh ho, Kunti, no talking problems now, just party planning for the bitter – what did you call it? Bitter what?'

'Bunch of bitter biddies ...'

'What's a biddy, exactly?'

'An older woman but in a really nice way, a fun way?'

'Ha ha! Let's have a Bitter Biddies Bunch!'

'Yes, yes, lovely name.'

'So should we agree that we'll order food from outside?'

'Yes, pizzas ....'

'And kebabs.'

'But with Satya's cakes!'

'Yes, yes, I'll ice BBB on the top of the cake!'

Loud raucous laughter rang out. Then Kunti came up with another suggestion. 'What should we do for entertainment?'

'What, you don't call this entertainment?'

'Oh ho, but for the inaugural party we should do something special, no?'

They all got to thinking. What would make it special, something that would live up to the newly christened group?

'Let's watch a movie.'

'Or movies all night long, since we don't have to go home.'

'Hai no, that's so boring. I will just fall asleep in the middle of it.'

'We could play some party games.'

'Hain hain, that's so much fun.'

'Like what?'

'How about like passing the parcel?'

'Yes, with funny punishments!'

'Oh that is a good idea.'

'Accha, I think that we should have some drinks – no tea shee for us, we are going to have real drinks. Who drinks what, tell me? Then I'll organize it from the canteen.'

'I like a little whiskey.'

'Haw! Kunti, I never knew that!'

'I don't know what I like, I've only had brandy and that just went up my nose.'

'Nowadays many women drink vodka with some juice or something.'

'Yes, that sounds nice, I don't want anything too bitter.'

'Oh ho, then you can't come to the Bitter Biddies Bunch!'

'Yes, then we should have Gin and Bitters!'

'How about wine? I believe there are some good wines in India now.'

The laughter and suggestions came pouring in on a wave of enthusiasm.

'We'll need some snacks for our drinks. Should we get some chips?'

'Hai yes, but we'll get halwai waley wafers, not these Lay's-shays, they have no taste.'

'Yah, really, just pheeka.'

'Let's get some kebabs also for snakes.'

'Ho, ho, it's not snakes, Satya, its snacks.'

'No, no, I say, let's have snakes only!'

'Hai, Satya, make those lovely sausage rolls you did that time. Delicious they were. She made a pastry.'

'Chee, sweet sausages?'

'No, no, not sweet pastry, bhai, you know that pie crust type pastry. Then she rolled little sausages into them and baked them. What did you call them, Satya?'

'Pigs in blankets.'

'Hai, cho chweet!'

'Oh, I wouldn't mind a pig in *my* blanket, sometimes!'

'Cheeeee!' They all shrieked.

Suddenly Tosh noticed that Kunti had gone all quiet.

'Kya hua, Kunti, all well?'

Kunti started then, and surprisingly, she began to blush – going a bright crimson.

'Arrey, arrey, what has happened?'

'Nothing,' said Kunti coyly. 'I've just thought of something. You know, it's Satya's seventieth birthday that weekend. I've just thought of something special. But it's going to be a surprise.'

'Oh!'

'Haw! I forgot, I can never remember birthdays.'

'No, yaar, I'd rather forget that I'm entering my seventies.'

'No, no, it's a great occasion.'

'What have you thought of Kunti, tell na?'

'No! It's a surprise.'

And although they all tried to persuade her, Kunti was determined to keep her surprise strictly a secret until the party.

13

A few days later, Satya and Sheila were planning and preparing for the weekend. All of them were really looking forward to it. Phone calls had abounded, with prolific suggestions to make it more fun.

'I wonder what Kunti has got up her sleeve – can you guess?' asked Satya, who hated secrets and was all agog for this one. Especially since it was going to be a birthday surprise for her. She'd never had much celebrating of her birthday as a child, because her parents didn't believe in it. And then as a teacher, she would dread her birthday, because it meant forking out a treat for the staff room. It left her with no extra money to buy something for herself, as she often planned.

'Kyun, Sheila, can you guess what Kunti is planning?'

'No,' said Sheila slowly, lost in thought. Annu had called earlier that morning and Sheila had been a bit preoccupied since then.

'What's the matter Sheila, everything ok?'

'I'm just wondering what Annu has to say. It sounded like something important when she called. I've been wracking my brains about what it could be, but she refused to give me a hint over the phone.'

'Maybe she's expecting a baby?'

'Hai, how lovely that would be.'

But when Annu came, flustered and late after having been stuck in traffic for over an hour, it wasn't a baby she'd come to announce. From the look on her face, Satya saw she did indeed have something important – and perhaps not all together pleasant – to say. Satya excused herself and stepped out for a walk. She had a niggling worry that perhaps Annu was not happy with the fact Satya was moving in on a permanent basis. Was that what she had come to discuss?

'I can't blame her,' Satya thought. 'After all, she may feel that I could, you know, lay claim on the house or something. It's not unheard of. After all if, God forbid, Sheila was to go before me, then I would be the occupant of the house. Not that I would, but I suppose, theoretically, I could claim the property. Or even just influence her mother ....'

Satya chewed her lips worriedly: was she being too hasty in giving up her flat of so many years? Suppose Sheila and she had a falling out, what then? Sheila would not be affected, but where would it leave Satya? But she was so happy, just so happy to be here, surely nothing like that would happen? She could just keep the flat on and stay here, but that would be such a waste and Sheila would surely mind it. But suppose, just suppose the unthinkable happened and Sheila passed on before, then where would that leave her? Annu would want the house back. Would Satya be homeless?

But back at the house, Annu was not worried at all about Satya Aunty coming to stay. As Sheila had predicted, that news was a source of joy. It was a comfort that her mother would have company. The reason she wanted to talk to her mother was both good and bad.

'Ma,' she said, 'I have good news and bad.'

'Oh please, tell me, tell me quickly.'

'We've been transferred; Sonjoy and I have got a posting in Kolkata. In a hospital there. It's a good job, a great pay-hike, lots of perks. One of these new hospitals that are opening up.'

'Wow, Annu, that's very good news, I'm so happy for you beta. But what's the bad news, then?'

'We have to go away, see, we ... we can't leave you. Please Ma, will you come with us?'

'Leave, leave here?'

'Hain ma. What else to do, no? Sonjoy and I ... we, we were thinking, should we sell this house and you come and stay with us?'

'That's the bad news, why?'

'Oh Ma, we'd love for you to stay with us, you know that. But I also know that you love this house a lot, everything in it. I know that you and Baba built this with a lot of love and care.'

'Yes, yes, that is true.'

'I also know that you love your independence and enjoy being here, you have your life, your friends, your routine. That's the bad part, that you'll have to leave it.'

'Hmm. You and Sonjoy both feel this way?'

'We actually considered not taking the job there, just so that we don't disrupt your life for the sake of ours, but we'd really like to go. Sonjoy's parents are there and it would be nice to be close to them. In fact, maybe we can stay with them. But we can't leave you here in this huge house on your own.'

'Beta, I wouldn't be on my own. I'd be with Satya ...'

Sheila stopped, suddenly thinking of Satya, not herself ...

'Oh my god! Satya! How can I do this to her? Just when I've made this offer to her, how can I suddenly tell her that I've changed my mind?'

'I know Ma, I'm sorry this has come now, and so soon after Baba too. But we've thought about it and feel it would be best if you came with us. If not, we think you could sell this place and move to a flat in DLF or somewhere.'

'Why?'

'We'd just feel safer with you there, things like electricity, water, security, these are all issues taken care of for you.'

'But what about my friends, they'd find it so far – and then the Ram Sharnam, I wouldn't be able to go. I don't know Annu, let me think about it. Right now I know that I'd be happier here on my own, or rather, with Satya. Yes, I'd rather be here than in some fancy-shansi DLF flat.'

'Theek hai, Ma. Don't take a decision now, think about it. I know this is not easy and has not come at a good time for you, but ....'

'Nahin, beta, look, we'll do whatever you and Sonjoy feel is all right.'

'Yes, but I'd also feel very guilty disrupting your life.'

'Chalo, we'll think about it, but I'm not yet going to say anything to Satya. And by the way, how come you've not brought me any laddoo or mithai to celebrate your new jobs?'

'Oh Ma ...,' Annu hugged her mother. She had been dreading this conversation, knowing her mother valued her independence and had a well-established life with her special circle of friends. She knew it wasn't really fair that she should be the one to disrupt things, especially now, just when – with her father's passing – it would have freed Sheila to lead a more carefree life. She also knew if they stayed with Sonjoy's parents it would be a difficult transition for her own mother. She would be the daughter-in-law's mother: which meant she'd have to be very careful. Sort of walking on egg-shells. It was sweet of Sonjoy to offer that she come live with them. But perhaps, one of these builder flats would be a better idea.

Annu was gone by the time Satya came back from her walk. She found her friend in a decidedly pensive mood. She was worried – perhaps her instinct had been right. She could also make out a false cheer in Sheila. Finally she could stand it no longer and burst out, 'Is it about the house?'

Startled, Sheila said, 'How did you know?'

Satya – her worst fears confirmed – spoke in a rush of words. 'Oh Sheila, don't worry about it. Of course she wasn't comfortable with this arrangement. See, I myself said that you should check with her before we decided. Not to worry, straight after this weekend plan, I'll move back. I should have foreseen this. Oh dear, I hope she doesn't think of me badly. You know I would never do anything to harm her or your interests.'

'What? What are you talking about, my dear? I don't understand at all. This has nothing to do with you, bhai, where did you get that idea?'

'Didn't she come to say that she was uncomfortable with me moving here on a permanent basis? You only said just now, that it was something to do with the house. What else could it be?'

'Oh ho, Satyaji, this has really nothing to do with you, at least, not directly. For the record Annu is very, very happy you are here with me. I knew she would be. I'd told you.'

'Then?'

'Oh, I thought I wouldn't say anything to you right away, at least till I've given some thought to it. But chalo, now this has come up, I may as well ...'

She told her all about Annu and her husband's planned move out of Delhi. And of course, about their plans for the sale of this house. As she listened, Satya's heart was breaking; for just a brief little while, it had all been so glorious. For once she had thought the rest her life would be full of companionship, the one thing she'd missed so much. But now, now that dream would remain just that, a dream. But she kept a brave face, even a happy one, congratulating Sheila on her children's new jobs.

'I don't know, Satya, how can I think of selling this place? Oh I know, it has so many problems. It's old fashioned, it has so many cracks and leaks and of course, it's much too big for a single person. I did tell her we'd be the two of us, but still ....'

'Why not talk to some builders and see what they offer? Maybe it's a good idea after all. You'll be able to sell this for a good sum and then you'll be so comfortably off. Why, my dear, you could think of going off on cruises and all.'

Sheila got up with surprising swiftness. She walked to the drawing room wall, the one with a leak coming from the powder room. She put her hand on the mossy dampness and smiled at the flaking bits of plaster that came off in her hand. She put her cheek against the wall. Leaned into it and closed her eyes.

'Brick by brick ...,' she whispered. 'Brick by precious brick.'

Satya went up to her and put her hand on her shoulder, but Sheila was deep in her reverie. 'We went to the brick kilns and chose our bricks. We had a fresh batch fired, just for us. I examined almost every brick, every tile for the bathroom and kitchen.' She turned to lay her head on Satya's shoulder and continued. 'When the roof was being laid, Naren had to go out of town. He explained to me the mixture of cement and rori and what not that had to be mixed. He told me to keep an eye out as the contractor would try to shortchange us on the amount of cement he used. So there I was, trying to keep a watch. But I'd keep getting muddled. So then, I devised a method. Standing outside on the road next to the cement mixer, I would take a step forward for every cement bori that went in, then one step back when the mix was used. I was exhausted in the heat but I was sure that our roof was the strongest it could have been.'

'Wasn't there something you told me about the pipes?' said Satya. 'I can't remember the exact details but I remember laughing.'

'Yes, yes, of course. I had really forgotten that. Kya tha bhai, oh ho, I don't know if I can remember properly.'

'Nahin, nahin, come on, remember properly na, it was very funny how it happened. Something about two different kinds of pipes.'

'Hain hain, there was something, but hai, Satya I can't think of it.'

'Ok, but promise me you'll try and remember and tell, theek hai?'

'I promise. When we built this house, Satya, we never thought there would be a time when one of us wouldn't be there. Never thought about our deaths. Never thought the house, all our effort, would one day be killed ... you know, that's how it feels. Pulling down this house would be nothing short of murder. We're going to have to kill this baby of ours.'

Sheila went on. And on. Satya knew better now not to stop her. What could she have said anyway? This was not the moment to try and lighten the mood, to make her laugh.

Satya herself was in the throes of a restless helplessness. How was *she* going to be placed? Why was it suddenly others had become masters of her life, when she had been her own decision-maker throughout? She was suddenly able to understand more and more what Kunti said about having other's decisions impacting her life. And Satya wasn't even sure whether this was something she was happy or sad about. She was more confused than she'd been for a long time.

Eventually, Annu and Sonjoy came over with estate agents and brokers and builders. Each one made a bid. Even Slimy Sardar made a hefty offer. In fact, his was the best offer. Sheila sat quietly while the negotiations went on. Satya was careful to disappear altogether when it was all being discussed. For one thing she felt her presence was improper, and for another, she was sure she would burst into tears and make it more difficult for everyone. Annu had quietly come and apologized to her one afternoon. 'I'm really, really sorry aunty,' she said, 'I'm so grateful to you for having been with Ma and we could not have done this without you. It was such a lovely thought you would be staying with her. You know, she still hasn't decided one way or another, but if she does decide to stay in Delhi, instead of coming with us, then maybe you could stay with her in her new place, even? Would you?'

'Let your mother – and of course you – decide what's going to happen, then I'll see; after all, I lead such a simple life, I don't have many possessions, so I don't need to decide anything straightaway.'

She herself sensed some of the old bitterness creeping right back into her tone and voice.

As their weekend together approached, Sheila and Satya decided to put a determined end to the moroseness that had pervaded their mood since the whole house thing began.

'We're not going to let it spoil things for us, Satya, there is no need to share all this with the others, let's just try and have a good time.'

'Why only try, we *will* have a good time, a wonderful, lovely time.'

So Satya got busy with her baking. She was going to ice the cake with BBB for Bitter Biddies Bunch. Trying very hard to lift her own mood, Sheila suggested they make a welcome banner. Immediately Satya, who had made innumerable bulletin boards in her school, got the whole thing into motion. The two of them went to a stationery shop. There they bought a thermacol sheet, paints, crepe paper, glue, glitter and some colourful wrapping paper. At home, as they started designing the layout, Sheila said, 'Why should we call ourselves the Bitter Biddies? I don't think we're such a bitter bunch, do you?'

'You know, you're quite right, we're really not that bitter, a little, but considering everything ... yes, let's get a better name. Shall we ask the others?'

'Wait, how about the Bitchy Biddies Bunch?' they both laughed, feeling deliciously naughty.

'Oof, so bad you are, what will Tosh and Kunti think – we should ask them.'

'No, I say, we should leave it as a surprise. See, with a name like that we can be as bitchy as we like and shred everyone to pieces, we're only living up to our name!'

'Chalo, ok, let's do it. Let's really do it! Oh what fun! I'm sure Kunti will be fine with it, how many curses she's been using. But listen, if either of them –especially Tosh – objects, then it was your idea, ok? After that time, I'm not going to stick my neck out, theek hai?'

'Oh no, I'm not sharing my brainwave with you, I will take full credit for the brilliant name. I know, let's make badges also, like we used to for our secret clubs when we were girls!'

So the banner was put up, announcing the Bitchy Biddies Bunch. There was a badge for each one, saying B3, with little crepe paper whiskers. They had argued as to whether there should be cat's whiskers, like when you're, catty or dog-like whiskers for bitchy. Eventually, they looked like something in between.

The beds were laid, the DVD player head cleaned. Flowers were put in the bedrooms and living room. Candles were placed in the dining room and even perfumed candles in the bathrooms, 'for sexy baths,' said Sheila, now really pulling out all the stops. She put fresh scented handmade soaps, sachets of shampoos and mini toothpastes next to brand new toothbrushes. 'Oh ho, what a waste,' grumbled Satya, who couldn't begin to imagine such extravagance. 'They'll all bring their own toothbrushes, na.'

'Ok, so they won't be used, but it just looks complete, doesn't it?' And Satya had to admit that indeed it did.

On the day itself, the maids were asked to lay the table with the best china, the best table linen and Sheila even brought out her silver cutlery for the occasion. Then she told the maids to take the day and night off. 'You only need to come back tomorrow morning,' she told them. They had both decided the presence of the maids would inhibit their mood. The maids were truly surprised; they'd never seen their memsahib in a mood such as this before this other memsahib had come. And they'd certainly never had a night off when there was a party on. They'd worked extra hard, not got a night off! It was nice to see though, and they were happy to see her so carefree and light. In a fit of extravagance, as though she had caught the fever of it, Satya splurged by giving the maids money to go off and watch a movie in a hall, instead of the usual DVD they watched sometimes when memsahib went to sleep early. What a treat! They certainly changed their minds about Satya memsahib now.

Sheila and Satya dressed up for the occasion. Sheila in a lemon and silver gauzy chiffon leheriya sari and Satya in an ethnic salwar kameez in black and red, with mirror work on the dupatta. Something she had bought once for a founder's day in her school, but never worn after – there had hardly been an occasion for her to dress up. She put on her usual plain gold ear studs, but when Sheila saw her, she immediately took her into her bedroom and got out some tribal jewellery, chunky and very ethnic. 'This will go better with your outfit,' she said, settling on a pair of silver dangler earrings and a long, thick silver chain with big pendant. Then she made Satya wear a bunch of pretty silver bangles. 'It's your birthday, I want you to have these,' she insisted.

She herself had worn only a rice pearl necklace with little earrings to match and would not be persuaded to don more, although Satya said that she'd feel overdressed if she was the only one with so much jewellery.

Finally, all was ready. They were so excited as they waited for the others, that Sheila suggested that they have a 'medicinal dose of vodka' while they waited. Tosh had already delivered it to their house, a few days earlier. Mixed with the orange juice, it tasted quite nice and gave them both a nice warm, settled feeling. They were beautifully calm when, at last, the doorbell rang.

14

Tosh and Kunti came laden with bags; some held their personal things like nightclothes, toothbrushes and laxatives. Other bags contained more fun things for the weekend. And there was a big fancy gift bag from Tosh for Satya.

They shrieked when they entered the living room. Satya held her breath, would they object, or would they go along with the fun?

'Bitches!!!'

'Oh my god, do you know the last time I said "bitch" out loud?'

'When you told that joke, remember?'

'And when was the last time you said god and bitch in the same sentence?'

They were falling over themselves laughing. 'When did you decide this, you naughty, naughty girls?'

They really were girls now, not women in their sixties and seventies certainly not ladies, in the old-fashioned sense of the word. They were all dressed up, but this time for themselves, for each other, for the bitches that they were. They were delighted to know there would be no servants in the house to be self-conscious about.

As she dug in to see Tosh's gift to her, Satya started laughing. For out of the bag came a sexi-ish nighty and a more sober, but matching and elegant dressing gown. 'Oh ho, and who am I going to impress when I wear this?' she laughed gleefully, rushing over and hugging Tosh, whispering into her pearled ear, 'I've always, always wanted one of these, but never had the guts to buy it for myself, thank you, thank you.' She stroked the filmy fabric.

Satya went and brought out the welcome drinks they'd learnt from another episode of a television programme. As Kunti took the orange and red drink with a fancy straw and a slice of pineapple stuck on the rim, she laughed. 'What, Satya, no extra big bust line to show off this time with your drinks?' And the little tension Satya was carrying over from that time melted.

Kunti took a sip of the drink and hugged Satya. 'Mmmm, this is truly delicious. I hope there's some booze in it too?'

'Actually, no, there isn't, we weren't sure if you'd want it. So we've made it virgin ....'

'Virgin?! At this age – rubbish! Please seduce mine immediately!'

This, of course, brought a huge guffaw, Tosh was blushing hugely. 'Bhai, if this is how you all are going to behave, then I'm leaving!' she said, wiping tears of laughter from her cheeks. 'No, not because I don't enjoy the jokes, but because my glasses keep getting stained with my tears!'

The drink was doused with generous doses of vodka. The snacks were all non-vegetarian or deep fried. There were going to be no half measures this weekend.

As planned, they called for pizza with extra toppings and cheese and they also called for kebabs and rotis. Fish, mutton burra, chicken tikka, tandoori chicken, dal makhani, butter naan, the works. Their dentures were going to have to work very hard that night.

But when Sheila started burping and hiccupping at the same time, they decided that they needed some exercise in the form of games.

First it was passing the parcel. The music chosen was something Kunti's daughter-in-law had recorded for their weekend. It had the best of the latest Hindi movie and Punjabi bhangra tunes. The pillow as it was flung around, of course, knocked down a glass first. But luckily the glass was empty and landed on the carpet. So there was no harm done. A quick clean up and they were ready to go. As had been decided, they all had made up the forfeits. The first to get a punishment was Kunti, 'Hai, not fair, Sheila, I saw you pressing the remote just when it came to me!' But the punishment was something that she greatly enjoyed. She had to dance like Bipasha Basu in the Bidi song. Quickly, she opened her joora and tucked her best kanjeevaram sari into the waistband. Then she just took off, gyrating and doing her vulgar best. The others clapped along; Tosh took a ten rupee note from her bag and did a sarvarna over Kunti's head. The music started up again. This time it was Sheila's turn. Tosh had a forfeit for her. She had to sing an old Hindi movie song, something she did so very well. She sang gracefully, forgetting a word here or there, but being helped along by the others, as she forgot the lyrics. Her eyes were moist as she finished, remembering the songs she sang for Naren since the time they'd first met. But she didn't let her tears fall. The music started up again. Someone's maid was mimicked, a gidda was danced and some more songs were sung. They were at the end of their prepared forfeits, but still having a whale of a time. They started making them up on the spur of the moment, depending on who was left holding the cushion. When Satya was to be given a punishment, Kunti immediately demanded she do another imitation of Nigella. Amid much laughter Satya started, but Kunti stopped her, insisting she first stuff something into her shirt, 'You are too flat-chested, my dear, kuch maal to dikhao!' In revenge, when it was Kunti's turn, Satya made her do an imitation of herself shouting at Satya, the last time she'd done her Nigella impersonation. Kunti hammed it up completely, throwing in some full-blooded Punjabi swear words, cursing mothers and sisters. Tosh was turning redder and redder until it was her turn and they all made her shout swear words on the top of her voice. They finally stopped only when they were too hoarse and their sides ached from so much laughter.

Food arrived. As per the plan, they all pooled in the money and all spending was to go out of that. They were hungrier than they'd been in a long time. The fun, the anticipation and the company had fired up their appetites. The food was great, just what they'd wanted, for it was far from the bland, low oil, low salt, low taste food they had all taken to eating. There were lots of leftovers, despite their best efforts. So they cleared it up, promising that it would be demolished the next day.

'Bhai, I need another drink!' And soon, their glasses were refilled, the vodka rapidly diminishing.

'Arrey, Kunti, you promised us a surprise, ab tell us now what it is?'

'Before I do, I think we'll have to have one more drink.'

'No, no,' they all protested, 'enough, enough.'

'Can't have another, I'll be completely drunk.'

'Then, sorry, no surprise. One more drink and you'll get such a surprise, the kind that you've probably never had in your whole life – unless some of you have, on the sly.'

So, the vodka was pressed into service once again. And although the protests were loud and long, their glasses were soon emptied.

'Oh, oh, I'm going to be so unhappy tomorrow.'

'Arrey, kal ki kisne sochi hai?'

'Enjoy now, pay later, that's my motto.'

'That's your motto in life?'

'No, no, bhai, only for tonight, but maybe I'll extend it for the full weekend.'

'Excellent – all those who vote to elect this motto for the Bitchy Babes, hands up.'

'Bitchy Babes, what happened to the Biddies?'

'Oh, one and the same baby, one and the same!'

'So, now can we have your surprise Kunti? If you make me have one more drink, I'll sleep through it, whatever it is.'

'And I'll pee through it …,' laughed Tosh, blushing furiously at the use of such a word, pressing her thighs together, realizing she really did need a visit to the loo.

'Wait, wait, I have to go to the toilet, don't you?'

'Yes, yes, fellow Bitches, it is time for a pee break, but make it quick.'

Finally they were ready, and Kunti instructed, 'Accha, theek hai, now, all of you sit over here on this sofa, leave place for me, ok?' She went off to her bags and pulled out a plastic packet. 'Sheila, where are your TV and DVD remotes?'

'Oh ho, is it a movie? I don't want to see a movie, bhai, I can't concentrate at all, right now.'

'When you see what I have, let me see if you can get your eyes off the screen. Be patient.'

Finally, after a few arguments about how to go from the dish TV to AV, which remote would control what, they managed to get it started. Kunti refused to let anyone look at the cover of the CD. 'It'll give away the surprise. Satya, be a good girl and make sure all the curtains are drawn.'

'They're closed, bhai.'

'Just make sure once, na.'

'This had better be good,' they said as the film started.

And then the shriek that went up could have woken up the whole neighbourhood. For on the screen, a good looking blond man had begun to take his clothes off. *All* of them. Until he was stark naked, in all his glory. And what glory!

'Hai hai, what's this Kunti, yeh kya ley aayi?'

'What's the use of a naughty girl's weekend if we don't have any pornography?' They protested, they play-plummeled her, but the fact is, they didn't take their eyes off the handsome man as he went into the bathroom and got into the shower where a beautiful, very well-endowed girl was soaping herself.

They'd never seen anything so explicit. None of them. Some had seen some 'hot' movies, but nothing as graphic as what they were watching now. Satya, who had never ever seen a naked man before, insisted all the lights be put off so no one could see how eagerly she was watching.

Occasionally, they'd shriek again and shut their eyes, but quickly open them again, lest they miss some of the action. There was plenty of action.

At one point, they insisted on pressing the pause button and refreshing their drinks. And also catching their breaths.

'Too good, too good, Kunti, what a brilliant idea this was!'

'Where did you get them? Don't tell me you called for them from the CD rental place?'

'Are you mad? Bhai, there have to be some advantages of living with your sons!'

More shrieks followed this announcement. 'Do they know, don't tell me you asked them?'

'Of course not, but I was sure they had them. Some days, they insist on sending the children to sleep with me, I knew, after all, what else must they be up to?'

'So you stole them?'

'Of course! You know, I had to do it before they left, otherwise they would have locked up their cupboards. Arrey, such an adventure it was to get them.'

'And they have no idea?'

'None whatsoever – at least, I hope not!' There were squeals of laughter as they restarted the movie. This time there was a black man who was very, very well endowed. As the movie went on, episode after episode, they all divided the porn stars amongst themselves.

'I'll take the black one, never tried that flavour before!'

'Hai, cheeee! Dirty girl.'

'Ok, so you decide on yours.'

'I like the blond one, so handsome.'

It was two in the morning before they finally decided to stop the movie show. But as they were heading off to their bedrooms, Kunti had another surprise.

'Satya, don't think I've forgotten your birthday present.' She went over to her suitcase and pulled out a gift-wrapped box.

'See, I've got it specially gift wrapped for you!' Satya was carefully trying to ease off the scotch tape, so used was she to saving wrapping paper. But Kunti made her tear it off, she was too eager to show everyone the brilliantness of her gift. The box was one for a massage and heat pad.

'Oh,' said Satya, a bit disappointed; after all the excitement of the pornography, it wasn't very appropriate to be reminded that she was now seventy and needed such practical gifts.

'Open the box, silly,' Kunti was almost hopping from one foot to another in her impatience.

As the lid fell away, there was more shrieking. For inside, nestled a whole stack of *Playboy* magazines!

'Oh my god, oh my god, oh my god!!!!' was all Satya could say. 'Hey bhagwan, kitni badmaash hai tu, Kunti!'

Well, each of them got one copy of *Playboy* to take to bed with them. None of them objected, none of them shrieked anymore. They slept late and awoke later than they had in a very long time.

The weekend passed like a blissful dream. There were their cakes, there was more food, more vodka and most important, more movies and magazines. Kunti had really raided the larder!

Annu, who had planned to drop in and meet the aunties, was called up and told, please don't come. 'Oh,' said Sheila, 'this old house must be so happy to have had such a time. It has been witness to too much sadness recently, I'm sure it is smiling too.'

Finally it was Monday morning and the weekend was at an end. By this time, they had had a dance party, put streamers up and had drunk two bottles of vodka and several beers. Kunti had decided to go off to spend some days with her Mamaji in Noida, although now she was regretting her decision. 'It's been so much fun, I wish I'd just decided to stay on.'

'Stay there a bit and then come back,' they offered. They tried to persuade Tosh to stay on, too. After all, she did not have any commitments. But she said that she needed to get back. But as they all agreed, this was something they had to repeat sometime, it had been just so much fun.

Satya and Sheila were quiet, for who knew whether this good old house would be sold by the time they got around to a next time.

15

As Annu and Sonjoy's plans crystallized, it was decided they would stay with his parents in Kolkata. Sheila concluded it would be best for her to sell this house, as they wanted, and then move into a flat on the outskirts – either in Gurgaon or Noida. One that had all the amenities. She would get herself a new car and a full-time driver to compensate for the fact she would be living further out of the city. Satya had decided not to release her flat as yet. After the initial euphoria she realized she would probably feel too dependent and insecure if she did not keep a place in her own name. Sheila was not very happy with this and thought she would somehow persuade her later on.

Slimy Sardar, who – on Annu's request – was now referred to as Mr Inderjit, was asked to draw up a proposal for the purchase of the house, while Sheila went to the bank and got all the documents and papers together. She broke down when she saw her husband's handwritten master list of papers. How meticulous he had been. How easy he had made it all for them. The process of packing had to be started. Sheila was given boxes so that she could sort things out. 'Ma, remember, you're going to be moving to a smaller place, so you will have to get rid of a lot of stuff.' Sheila smiled and nodded, although the words 'get rid of' cut her to the quick. It was her life they were talking of here, a life full of memories.

Finally, finally, the day arrived. Mr Inderjit was coming to give the bayana, the earnest-money to confirm the sale was on. Satya had said that she would go to her flat for the night so as to leave the family to do this. But Sheila requested she stay with her. 'Please, without you, I won't be able to carry it out. I'll need you once I've signed the papers,' she said, her voice already quavery with emotion. So Satya helped serve the tea, then sat tensely in the guest bedroom, watching television with her finger on the mute button. 'Why am I so tense?' she asked herself. But she was and she knew, in her bones, that it was her home, her future being decided out there too, and she felt helpless for it.

Then she could hear the sound of crying. She sat ramrod straight. She loved Sheila so much, like the sister she never had. She wished she could rush right out and put her arms around her. What, oh what, was going on?

She could hear chairs scraping. The meeting was over. The house was sold. The door opened, goodbyes were being said. But Sheila was still crying. What had happened? What, oh what, was it? Had Annu and Sonjoy really forced her to do it, so obviously against her wishes? Satya was trembling when Annu finally came in. Her cheeks were wet. She held her hands out to Satya. 'She wants you,' was all she said, but when Satya took her outstretched hands, they were icy cold. She wanted to ask if it was all over, but she did not have the courage to hear the truth.

Sonjoy was standing awkwardly, patting a sobbing Sheila on the shoulder, holding a cup of tea in his other hand. Annu left Satya and rushed back to her mother, 'Ma, amma, please Ma, please, look I'm sorry, we're really very sorry. We thought it was for the best. You should have told us how you felt, Ma. Please Ma, don't cry now.'

Satya was confused. She couldn't figure out what had happened. She looked at Sonjoy, he looked back and shook his head. What did that mean?

'Oh Satya, Satya, I couldn't do it. I couldn't sign the papers. The house means too, too much to me. I couldn't sell it. I'm so sorry Sonjoy, I'm so sorry to have put you through all this.'

'It's all right Ma,' he said. 'It doesn't matter, I wish you'd told us how you felt. We didn't mean to put you through so much misery.'

'I myself didn't know how I felt. I thought it would be all right. Of course, it would be hard, but I thought, when the time came ... but oh, I couldn't, I couldn't.'

So the whole idea of what to do with the house, with Sheila, hung in the balance again. What was going to happen? Finally, Sheila gathered up all her thoughts, packed them tight with courage and came out with what she wanted.

'I cannot leave this house, Annu. I won't see it sold in my lifetime. It means too much to me. When I'm gone, then you are at liberty to do what you want with it.'

'Ma, we're not doing this for ourselves, you know that.'

'I know, I know, but as long as I am able to decide what is best for me, it is best I take that decision.'

'Of course, that's we want too, Ma.'

'Fine, then I want you to listen carefully: I have had these thoughts for some time, but I thought I could adjust, but now I realize I don't want to. Now, here is what *I* want to do.' Her back was straight, her shoulders squared, not in tension, not in aggression, but with a confidence that seemed to make her glow.

'As long as I am able to lead my own independent life, I would like to do so. I have been very happy, these past few weeks, although I know this sounds harsh so soon after your father's passing away. But it is a fact that I – we – have been happy – happier – than we have been in a long time. I don't want to give that up as yet. I don't want to give up this house either. As long as I can, I will live here. Then if, god forbid, I become an invalid, unable to look after myself, then, Annu, you are free to decide what to do with the house and what to do with me. I promise to have no objections then.'

'Of course, Ma, we respect that.'

'Also, I understand you have had concerns about me staying here alone, I also have those concerns. But, if Satya agrees, I would be very grateful if she would continue to live here on a permanent basis. Satya, I also want to request you to give up your flat or at least put it on rent and save that for yourself. For your future. So that when I am gone from here, in one way or another, you will have something to fall back on.' Satya started to say something, but Sheila continued. 'By the grace of god, I have enough put aside, more than enough for the two of us. Sukh naal, Sonjoy and Annu are doing very well for themselves, and now with their new jobs, it will be even better. They do not need anything from Naren's insurance or pension, isn't that right beta?'

They both nodded. 'So Satya, it would make me much happier for you to be able to save your money. Is that all right by all of you? Satya do you need time to think this over?'

Satya felt a bit awkward: she did not really need to think, but she did not want to appear too eager either, so she just nodded, agreeing to this very generous offer. 'If it's all right with you, Annu, Sonjoy?'

'Of course aunty, we'd be very happy, very grateful if you'd be here with Ma,' said Annu and Sonjoy nodded too.

'Thank you, Satya, I'm really happy. Now, if you could excuse us for just a little while, I need to talk to Annu and Sonjoy.' Satya left them.

Sheila took a deep, deep breath. She asked them to sit on either side of her. She held their hands.

'I'm really sorry, my dear dear children, to have put you through all of this. The fact is I did not know how hard it was going to be, I wasn't happy, but I thought I could do it.'

'It's ok Ma.'

'I want to say two things. First, in my will, if you both agree, I'd like to put aside some money for Satya. She has been like a lifeline for me and I know she has led a hard life of financial strife.'

'She is your very dear friend and it would be so much like you to be able to do that. We support you completely.'

'Thank you. Now, for the second thing. After having nursed your father through such a long period of illness I know how draining it can be, not only for the one who is looking after, but even for the one who is being looked after. I often felt when he looked at me, he was begging me to let him go. But, for my own selfish reasons, I couldn't, I wouldn't. Now, I need you to promise me if I were to be terminally ill, you will not battle to keep me alive. I want you to let me go … please.'

Annu was crying; she rested her head on her mother's lap and wept: for her father, for this precious birth house of hers she had come to the verge of losing, for her mother's strength, for the thought that one day she would lose her too.

Without a word Sheila just stroked her head for a few minutes, before adding, 'Sonjoy, if – when the time comes – you as a doctor are able to donate my eyes, or my kidney or liver, or whatever, I would be very proud and happy to do so. Donate my whole body for research. I'd rather that than having myself cremated. But you both have to be okay with this.'

Although he was not a person given to a show of affection, this last caused Sonjoy to put his arm around her shoulder and give her an awkward hug. 'Yes, Ma.'

16

A fortnight later, Satya decided to sell her house. She had quietly been to some old-age homes in the city and found she would be better off living there if the need ever arose in the future. Her own flat, perched at the end of so many stairs, would no longer be practical. She found a buyer quite easily. In fact, it was Gopalji, the sweet old man who lived downstairs. He was happy to buy the flat just upstairs for his son. And so, it was time for Satya to release her house. Over the past few days, she'd been coming over to pack up. Most of her things had already gone to Sheila's – or rather, to her new house, as Sheila insisted she call it.

As she climbed up the stairs one last time, she found she had to pause several times to catch her breath. How was it that it had never seemed so difficult before? She finally made it to the top floor, heaving. She opened her cupboard and saw herself in her mirror. She had put on weight. There was no doubt about it. Her arms were plumper, her stomach rounded outwards instead of sinking in as though to meet her backbone. For the first time in her life, she had put on weight. She leaned in closer and examined her face. A radiant smile beamed back at her. Her fingers ran over her face, over skin that was softer, less lined, less wrinkled than it had been in the last few years. 'You're younger!' she smiled to her reflection. 'You're beautiful. You're not a DDA yellow anymore. You're daffodil yellow, or even better – sunshine yellow, glowing!'

The boxes and suitcases were mostly packed. There were piles of things to be given away. The mattress, the buckets, the mugs, the soap dishes, the old durries, bedcovers and curtains, some dishes and utensils from the kitchen. The sum total of her life was boxed into one room. There was surprisingly little. She had arranged with Sheila's driver to fetch a tempo to take the things away; now she wondered if it wasn't a waste. After all, there wasn't so much to take. Going through the flat one last time, checking that nothing important had been left behind, Satya was stabbed by a pang of separation. It was unexpected; she'd thought the walking away would be easy; she was leaving of her own free will, towards a better life. Yet, leaving a home of thirty-six years was surprisingly hard. She lingered in her bedroom, thinking of the dreams she'd dreamt there. Dreams of men who would fall in love with her, make gentle love to her, start a family with her, be her companion in her old age. Well, she thought to herself, I didn't find a man, but in a way I do have a family now, a companion for my old age. I have a chance at a new life.

As she got the cheque and cash payment from the sweet, little old man, she was startled when he suddenly took her by the hand and his face crumpled. They'd had a polite and neighbourly relationship, getting milk and sugar from each other when the need arose. And when his wife died some fifteen years ago, she was the one to bathe the body and send food over. But nothing more than that. He seemed to be eager to say something, but obviously his heart was so full he was choking on his words.

'Bhai sahib,' Satya began, trying to help him as his mouth opened but no words came. 'Bhai sahib, you have been such a pillar of strength and comfort to me.'

'No ...,' he choked. 'No.'

She did not know what he meant by this or how to respond, so she waited.

Finally he lifted one hand off her's while tightening his grip with the other. He wiped his eyes under his smeary glasses and they fell back askew on his nose, but he didn't seem to notice. 'It's you,' he whispered, whimpered almost, 'it's you who has been a source of strength to me. With you here, I never felt alone. I thought, I thought, I never thought of the possibility that you would go ....' He left her hand now and looked up at her like a puppy, pleading with her not to leave him alone. She was caught completely off guard. This was a surprise indeed.

'Bhai sahib, I'm not going away, na, I'm just shifting, not even so far away. I will come to see you, sometimes, ok?'

He grabbed at her hand again, as though he might drown in his sorrow. 'P-p-promise? You promise?' he pleaded.

'Yes, yes, I promise, I will.' And suddenly, he leaned towards her and laid his head lightly on her chest. She was taller than him. Then he straightened up, both pulling away in embarrassment.

Awkwardly, not knowing how else to comfort him, she straightened his glasses, turned and left, going as quickly down the stairs as she dared. She felt oddly elated, pleased at how much she suddenly meant to so many people.

17

Sheila was at the front porch when she arrived. She had made a special effort to welcome her. The clothes that she'd already brought over were hanging neatly on new hangers in her closet. There were flowers and sweet smelling pot pourri in the bathroom. On the bathroom shelf stood a row of special cosmetics – shampoos, conditioners, brand new exotic soaps, hand cream and body butter. On her very own dressing table, stood a pot of cream and a talcum powder, nail file and clippers. While Sheila had given Satya the spare guest room, Satya often just slept in the big double bed with Sheila. And Sheila was always grateful for it. Then, over their weekend, Satya had moved most of her things into Sheila's bedroom to make room for Tosh. And since then, she'd never slept in her own room again. Although she still used the closets in the other room for her clothes and the bathroom as her own. And she slept there in the afternoon.

New sheets were laid on their bed now. A new reading light especially for her had been installed as she liked to read at night. Along with the regular food, there was also some saffron rice, an auspicious welcome-home dish. Satya felt enveloped by love, warm and wanted. She set up her god-pictures in a corner of the bedroom and lit an incense stick immediately, thanking god for having given her such a friend, such an opportunity.

As Friday approached, Tosh asked if Sheila felt up to coming out now. 'If you'd like to, then we can have our get-together at my place.' Sheila was more confident now, now that she had managed to get things straightened with Annu and Sonjoy. Now that the house was safe. Now that she had Satya. She felt ready to step out into the world.

So, Friday morning, Kunti came by and picked up Sheila and Satya on the way to Tosh's house. 'I tried to call Tosh to ask if she needed anything, but both her numbers have been engaged all morning.'

'Really? That's strange, she's not one to chat too long on the phone.'

Sheila looked out of the window as they passed through the market. It felt good to be out, to be free. She asked for the airconditioner to be put off so that she could roll her window down and feel the breeze on her face. It felt so good, so alive. It had been a long time since she'd felt the breeze on her face, at least it felt like that. She felt alive at this moment. This very moment.

When they got to Tosh's they found a very sad looking stranger there. She was about their age, could have been younger, except for the deep wrinkles on her face and the dark circles under her eyes. Tosh introduced her.

'This is Puja, my cousin. She's staying with me for a while.' Tosh introduced the three of them, but they noticed that Puja wasn't really taking in their names or faces, or anything much.

'Behenji, I'll go and lie down, you go ahead.'

'Are you sure, Gudiya? You're most welcome to join us, isn't she, girls?'

'Of course.'

'It would be a pleasure.'

'Yes, you don't need to go away on account of us.'

But Puja shook her head and walked away slowly, bowed down as though the weight of the world was upon her.

Tosh watched her go and then whispered, 'Oh ho, I was hoping she'd stay and cheer up a bit.'

'What's happened to her? Not well?'

'Arrey, what a sad life the girl's had, what to say. She was married to my cousin; actually, she's my in-law. But we had no idea that he was beating her up and torturing her all these years.'

'Hai hai.'

'She never told anyone. They got married in the States and then he came back here. But mostly all her family is there only, poor thing. He started drinking after it was found they could not have a baby. She went through all tests and everything was okay with her. He refused to go for any tests himself, but finally when she took a sample, they found he was nearly fully infertile. Instead of doing anything about it, he started drinking and of course, with that, came the beatings and abuse and torture and all.'

'And she never told anyone?'

There was a silent exchange of glances between Sheila and Tosh as they remembered Sheila's shameful secret – the day she had been slapped by her husband. Satya noticed it but decided to let it go.

'Never. Imagine! She suffered quietly, hardly going back to her home, hardly keeping in touch with any of us. Then he got sick, that thing in the liver from too much alcohol, kya kehtey hain usko?'

'Scilosis, or something like that.'

'It's cirrhosis,' corrected Satya, who knew a lot about diseases. 'So then?'

'I only found out by accident. I'd gone to get my BP and sugar test, and who do I see in the hospital but Puja, looking like such a wreck. I went up to her; first she pretended that she hadn't seen me, then that she didn't know who I was. But you know me. I wasn't going to just leave it at that. Then the poor thing broke down and told me the whole story.'

'Poor thing, and how is he now, recovering?'

'No, no, he died.'

'Oohhh.'

'No, no, from what all she's been telling me, it's just as well. He'd made her life hell. And the day I saw her at the hospital, she had just discovered that he had drunk away all their savings, he'd emptied out the locker, all her jewellery and had mortgaged the house.'

'And she never knew?'

'She never knew. She went to the bank to withdraw the money for his treatment, but there was nothing left. She's broke and no house even.'

'Now?'

'Anyway, he passed away. I've asked her to come and stay with me, aur kahan jayegi, bechari?'

'Hai, so good you are Tosh.'

'Then what, what else could I do? You all would have done the same thing.'

'She is looking so sad, so broken.'

'Tosh, call her out, ask her to join us, we don't have to play cards, let her just come out of her shell.'

'I'll ask, but I don't know, mostly she doesn't even want to sit with me.'

'Try and persuade her.'

Tosh did her best, but for now Puja was too shattered to join them. They had a subdued morning, talking softly, playing a little, but their hearts were not really in it. Tosh took some tea and snacks for her and came back out. As they were having their tea, a soft little sound made them turn around. It was Puja. She didn't say a word, but came and sat next to Tosh who slid over on the sofa to make room for her. She didn't meet anyone's eye after the shy little smile she gave them. And they, with all their years of training in handling awkward moments, continued to chat, covering up the silence with a warm blanket of comforting words.

'How was moving day, Satya?'

'You know, Sheila had made it so wonderful – I just don't know when she managed to do it. She got all these lovely cosmetics all laid out for me in my room, in the bathroom. Oh I feel like such a beauty queen.'

'Actually, I asked Tosh to buy the things, she knows much more about these things than I do. She got them and sent them over when you were out, so you have to thank her.'

'Oh my god, I feel so special, I tell you, it was just too much.'

'We thought you may need some bucking up after finally leaving your house after so many years.'

'Hai, should I tell you? Oof, it's so embarrassing, almost!' Satya began, blushing to her roots with the memory of her little neighbour's warm hands on hers, his head as it touched her breast.

'What? What?'

'Sounds juicy, tell na …?'

After a little persuasion and a decorous hesitation, Satya told them about his reaction to her leaving. 'I mean, it's not as if I had anything really to do with them. Just the usual you know, greeting on the steps, keeping the gas cylinder for the other if one was away, like that only. Then suddenly, all this hand holding-sholding … it was so embarrassing, I just didn't know what to do!' she giggled.

The others were dying to cheer and rag Satya, but for Puja's sake they kept their comments within the bounds of decent elderly old ladies' limits, gently teasing her that she should not give up such a good catch. Satya didn't divulge the head-on-her-chest part. That was too embarrassing, too special to talk about just yet.

The chatter was soothing for Puja, she listened to it passively. This seemed like such a sweet group, if only she'd allowed herself to have friends. But she'd been scared to let anyone into her sadness. She always thought if she didn't acknowledge it, if no one knew, then one day, miraculously, it would all disappear. But of course, it didn't.

She was really grateful to Tosh behenji; if it hadn't been for her, how would she have managed? Where would she be today? But she was troubled about what she should do now. She didn't have the strength to start all over again. And she had nothing to start from. Her own parents had died and she didn't want to go back to her in-laws. They were the only ones who had known about her husband's drinking problem; why hadn't they tried to help her then, or at least tried to help him? In any case, they were too old now. She had sent word to them about his death and they hadn't even come, nor sent her any word, let alone any condolence or offer of help.

'What will I do now? Where will I go?'

As though hearing her thoughts, Tosh patted her hand reassuringly.

18

Puja's presence and her sadness hung over the group darkly. It was Kunti who had everyone over at her house a week later. 'Tosh, bring Puja, if she'd like to come.' But Puja was not yet ready to leave her shell. 'We're going to have to do something to help her, you know,' said Kunti. 'We've all helped each other through so much. It would be a pity if we can't help her.'

Kunti's home was looking less neat and tidy, less prissy than they'd ever seen it. Normally she was a stickler for neatness, keeping her tiny crystal menagerie polished to a gleam. But today, there was a patina of dust – albeit a thin one – over her pride and joy.

No one mentioned it, but Kunti herself brought it up. 'You know, after that weekend I realized I waste so much time and energy on such rubbish; surely there is no harm in letting things be, how does it matter if a table is not completely straight, or the curtain not pulled all the way back? See? I've learned so much from you bitches!' How they laughed!

'By the way,' said Tosh, as they stopped for a break a while later. 'This pamphlet came in with my newspaper, look, I've brought it along.' She fished out a printed leaflet. It was for a day-long spa treatment. They pored over it: there were fruit peels and mud baths, and there were saunas and jacuzzis and all kinds of massages.

'I was thinking, let's all go for a day of indulgence, what do you say?'

This time even Satya, whose finances were no longer so stretched – now that she'd sold her flat – did not object. 'I only wish that Puja would come, though ...,' said Tosh longingly. It had been difficult for her to have such a depressing presence in the house. Not that she objected, or minded, but it was a downer nevertheless.

'Do you think it would help if one of us asked her?'

'I think it'd be better if we ask her to come over to one of our homes, or if we come to yours Tosh. I don't think this spa thing would be a good start. Dhirey dhirey she'll come out. Let her take it slowly slowly.'

So, a few days later, they left Puja at home and set off for the spa. Tosh was the only one who had any experience of this nature. Kunti had had massages from a malishwali who came home, but neither Satya nor Sheila had any experience. They were quite worried.

'So, tell me again, you have to take off all your clothes, all of them?'

'Arrey they've seen hundreds of bodies, its like going to the doctor.'

'Hai, hai, I've never been nanga-punga even in front of a doctor.'

'Haven't you gone for gynae checks?'

'Nahin, never, why should I? I've never had babies and all.'

'But have you never been for your check ups – that smear test, the mammogram, all that?'

'What's a mammogram?'

'It's like a photocopy of your breasts!' They laughed but Satya was quite horrified at the thought. No, she'd never had any of these tests. And in fact, neither had Kunti. But she chose not to mention it after Sheila bore in on Satya saying it was a very necessary part of being a woman. You could prevent cancer through early detection. 'I've got the best idea. I'm going to ask Annu to set up an appointment for all of us to go to the hospital for our check up. It'll be a healthy outing for us.' Sheila refused to be deterred, though they all shouted that it was too late for them to waste their time on any such checks.

In any case, it was now time for their spa treat. They were all excited, and nervous too, not knowing what they had really let themselves in for.

They were checked in by a lady in a starched white uniform; it was all so official looking that they felt more than a little overwhelmed. But it was only to be expected. Had they come just in ones or even twos, they would probably have run away. But each one gave the other the moral support to stay on and give this new experience a shot. They each chose what it was they wanted, like out of a menu card in a restaurant.

Tosh wanted a deep tissue massage, a fruit peel facial, a head relaxation oil massage and a reflexology session.

Kunti opted for a cellulite massage, a golden glow massage that used real gold in it, an ayurvedic head massage for hair fall and a reflexology session.

Sheila picked a relaxation massage, a mud pack, shirodhara, an ayurvedic massage on the head that involved dripping copious quantities of oil onto the forehead and a manicure and pedicure.

Satya was advised to have a full body massage to remove wrinkles through hydration and skin relaxation, a fruit facial and a manicure and pedicure. They tried to persuade her to dye her hair, She was the only one who had allowed herself to go grey; the rest of them had frighteningly black hair on rather wrinkled faces. But she balked at that and said she didn't want to get into a beauty trap that she'd be stuck with. The others liked this idea so much that they immediately decided that they would stop dyeing their hair as well. It didn't really matter how awful their roots looked for a while. 'No more beauty traps,' they swore.

They were to meet up in the sauna and jacuzzi after their individual treatments. They were all quite relieved when they were given beautifully soft white toweling bath robes so that they would not flap their flab about, or display their spare tyres or bony knees. It was not as difficult to get naked in front of the masseuses who seemed so relaxed themselves about the whole thing. Finally, the individual treatments were over and they met in the sauna-jacuzzi section. Now was the time of reckoning, for they would have to take their robes off in front of each other. Somehow it had been easier to do so in front of the bland-faced experts. In front of strangers.

Kunti was the one who decided they should take their robes off all together. So, on a one two three – with each trying to look away – they clambered into the swirling waters of the jacuzzi. Of course they sneaked peeks at each other, but this time around they decided that silence was the better part of valour. After all, each one was in no better shape than the other, so if they were to make jokes, well, there'd be enough to say about every naked body in there. But soon came another moment of reckoning: they had to get out. And that was a very funny sight. The dimpled bottoms, the breasts that could not be called sagging but well and truly sagged, almost covering up their belly buttons. Satya, with the wiry hair that had begun sprouting out of her chest and all of them with grey hair beneath, that belied the black above. Sheila had such a time laughing that she kept slipping back into the foamy water. 'Yours are like prunes!'

'Well, yours are like watermelons gone sad!'

'And hers are like walnuts, sorry that is the best I can do!'

They were giggling like children when some other ladies walked in. That sobered them up quickly as they hastily pulled on their robes.

Then they disappeared into the sauna. Now here they would be in full view of each other. But Sheila simply dropped her robe and lay down on the hot wooden slats with a sigh and that was a sign that the time for embarrassment was over and it was time to really let go.

'Ohhh, I love this,' sighed Satya, 'where has this luxury been all my life?'

They all agreed it was something they would repeat once a month.

'When was the first time you took all your clothes off in front of someone?' asked Kunti. Giggling, Tosh said that it was her wedding night. 'You took all your clothes off – first day itself?'

Satya was amazed at the conversation. She could not imagine what it must be like to be naked in front of a man. She could not imagine what a real naked man looked like, felt like. She listened to the conversation with rapt attention. In the warmth and naked intimacy of the sauna, they revealed more than they would have at any other time. It was a conversation they would refuse to acknowledge ever afterwards, in their fully clothed state. It was as if it had never happened. But it fired Satya's imagination even more than the films and magazines had done. Here was an intimacy that came as close as she would ever get to making love. A vicarious pleasure she had never envisioned before.

And finally, fruit juices were given to them to re-hydrate them post sauna. Then they went to pay their bills. That's when Satya had an even bigger surprise. It was her birthday present that they had all pooled in for – this day at the spa.

They were glowing with the treatment, the company and the general feel-good factor as they headed back.

Kunti sighed, 'Oh ho, how sad, my children are all coming back; I wish I could just come back with you two.'

'Why do you have to wait for them to go away. You can come when you like.'

'Yes, that's true, you should make yourself less freely available to them. Just say, "Sorry, I'm out for the weekend, I won't be here to babysit your bachaas!"'

'Ohh, hai what a delicious idea. Too good, too good. Imagine it, imagine me saying, "I'm sorry dahlings, you'll have to look after your own children yourself, I'm going off to the spa and a weekend of masti with my friends!"' She clapped her hands with delight at the thought.

And they made her practice this as a song as they stood outside the posh spa, not caring about the looks they were getting from the fancy, much younger women who walked in and out of there.

'I'm sorry, I'm sorry
I'm out for the weekend.
I'm sorry, I'm sorry
I'm off to the spa!'

They clapped and sang it, almost like a rap tune.

19

Tosh got home and found the front door locked. As she opened the door with her key, she was pleased Puja had managed to pull herself together enough to go out. She'd hated seeing her cooped up inside the house all day long. The house was dark inside, the curtains were all drawn. Tosh, still a-glow from her spa, went from window to window drawing the curtains, letting the late afternoon sunshine in, opening the window panes, letting the air freshen the inside.

And then – what a shock she got.

What a terrible shock!

For her beautiful, beautiful dahlias, the ones as big as dinner plates, kept safely in the back garden, were destroyed. Each one beheaded as though by a guillotine. She rushed out, with a cry of anguish. A mass of coloured petals lay like dead birds on the ground. Even buds – as yet unopened – lay like unborn children – dead – on the brown earth. Some of the pots had been upturned, with the careful mixture of leaf mold, bone meal and earth, with crushed egg shells and used tea leaves spilling out like a demolished rich chocolate cake. Who could have done this?

The maid would have gone by now. 'Puja, Puja …,' she shouted, but then realized she had gone out too.

Or had she? Had she …?

A sudden cold hand grabbed at her heart and sent a shiver of chill down her spine. 'Puja …?' She called out to her again. But there was no reply, no sign of life. Tosh flung her handbag on the couch and ran upstairs. Faster than she had for the longest time.

'Puja?' But Puja's door was locked. Locked from the inside. 'Puja, Puja, open up, please, please open the door, Puja!' Banging, banging on the door. Nothing. She rushed to her own room, wrenched open the door and then unbolted the door to the balcony, the one shared by both the upstairs rooms. She got to Puja's bedroom window and banged on the pane, shouting and hitting at the glass. She peeped in through the curtains, but she couldn't make out anything. What, oh what should she do? The driver! The driver hadn't yet given her the car keys.

Running back downstairs, almost falling over, she found the driver at the front door.

'Kya hua memsahib, you look ... what's wrong?'

'Puja, Puja memsahib ...,' she took him up to the locked door. Although he thought that maybe she was panicking too much, he tried to knock politely. Why was his memsahib getting so hysterical? She took him to the side of the balcony, making him look over the parapet at the destruction of her beloved flowers. It was then he realized that there was actually something wrong, she wasn't just panicking for no reason. 'Kya Puja memsahib ne yeh ...?' Tosh shook her head, she didn't know for sure if Puja had done it, but it did confirm something was wrong and that Puja had bolted her door from the inside and wasn't answering. She pointed to the glass pane of the window. 'Break it.' He rushed down, got the jack out of the car and ran back up. As she stood back, he swung it, smashing the glass at first contact. Then carefully, he removed the shards. Using the jack, he lifted the curtain, pushing it back to reveal ....

Puja lay on the floor, her legs at an awkward angle. Not a flicker of response to Tosh's shriek. Tosh was trembling, sinking to the ground. The driver quickly grabbed one of the plastic terrace chairs. He made her sit down, rushed downstairs, got her a glass of water and brought up the purse that she had flung downstairs. After making her drink the water, he asked her to call Sheila behenji. They needed some help. Tosh fumbled with the phone, trying to recall how to get the number from the mobile's phone book. The driver stood by, patient and collected. Then she got it; as she heard Sheila's voice, she broke down. 'Sheila, Sheila ... come, come quickly ...,' was all she could manage. The driver took the phone from her. He spoke to Sheila, explaining what had happened, asking her to come as soon as she could.

Sheila and Satya had not yet reached home. Sheila asked the driver to turn around and go to Tosh's. As she explained to Satya what had happened, Satya said, 'Sheila, call Annu or Sonjoy, they're doctors, they'd be the best people to have there.'

Soon the car was screeching to a stop at the front door. Almost at the same time, Sonjoy's car drove up to the gate. In the meantime, Tosh's driver had brought her downstairs and made her sit more comfortably. He had not let her enter Puja's room. He had then gone in through the broken window and opened the door to her room. He knew, from various television serials, he should not touch anything. He saw there was a letter on the table. And strips of medicine on the bedside table, about three of them. Empty. Let the others arrive, then they could decide whether and when to show the letter to Tosh.

Sheila and Satya sat with a shuddering, trembling Tosh as the driver took Sonjoy up to the room. Sonjoy found a pulse. The lady was not dead, but there was hardly any blood pressure and she was barely breathing. She'd taken sleeping pills. Was it all three strips, or had some been consumed earlier? The letter confirmed Sonjoy's worst fears.

Dear Tosh Behenji
I want to thank you from the bottom of my heart for having given me the happiest days of my life. I know that I have not been an easy presence in your home. But I want to tell you that I have never felt more secure, more wanted and cared for, not since I was a little girl.

You know that my marriage was a terrible one, that is not a secret from you. But you have often asked me why I never left and went back home. That part is a secret. I have never told this to anyone. It is too, too shameful. I wish I could have told someone before I die, but I couldn't bring myself to tell you. Now it is a secret that will go with me. All I can tell you is that I hated my father and my mother. My father used to beat me, he beat Ma also, I begged her that we should leave him. But she refused. Just let it keep happening. I don't know who I hated more. You will be shocked to read this. But believe me, I had my reasons. I don't think they really loved me either. In fact, I'm sure that they did not. Maybe that is why I was in such a hurry to get married and went ahead with the first man I was involved with, not waiting to find out more about him.

I am now at a dead end. I see no hope, no future. I have decided to end my life here and now. I cannot live with the guilt and shame and failure that my life has been.

I want to apologize to you for having done this in the one home, to the one person who really cared for me. But it is the only place from where I know my soul will go in peace.

To Whom It May Concern:
This is to confirm that I have taken this action on my own and no one should be held responsible for my taking of my own life.
Puja Sethi

Sonjoy scanned the contents of the letter quickly and then he put it into his pocket. Better keep this aside till Annu or someone was able to be with Tosh Aunty when she read it. Right now, he had to take Puja to the hospital. He picked up the empty strips of sleeping pills. If he called an ambulance, there was a likelihood of this becoming a police case. Yet, she needed to be rushed to the hospital immediately if there was to be a chance of saving her. There was no time to call for an ambulance. He called his colleagues at the hospital, told them to have the stretcher ready and the stomach wash at hand. He was going to bring her there in his own car. The driver and he carried Puja down together. The three women gasped as they brought her through the room where they sat. Satya leapt up to help them with the front door, the car keys, the car door. She ran in and got a sheet to cover Puja. 'Shall I come with you?' she asked, seeing Sonjoy's white face. He hesitated. 'Yes,' he said, it would be good to have her. 'Ask Ma to wait with Tosh Aunty though.'

Tosh's driver busied himself making tea for the ladies, praying that Puja memsahib would be all right. When he took the tea in, he found Tosh behenji and her friend sitting in front of the mandir in the hallway, praying. He went and joined them silently.

As Sonjoy drove, he asked Satya Aunty to dial Annu's number and told her of the situation. He asked her to come to the hospital and then she could go home and join her mother and Tosh Aunty. 'I think you should take a shot of something, to calm her down.' He said before ringing off.

Satya told him about Puja's stay. 'I wonder if we should have seen this coming?' she asked. 'She was very quiet, very depressed, Tosh behenji was very concerned for her, she kept trying to persuade her to come out with us, or at least join us when all of us came over.'

'You know, Aunty,' said Sonjoy, 'Annu and I really appreciate and almost envy your group of friends. You have such fun, you depend on each other, can call on each other any time. If Puja had allowed herself, if she'd been able to open herself up to you, who knows, maybe this would not have happened.'

'Kya patta, beta, it is such a pity that women suffer so much and don't tell anyone about their troubles. I wonder why she never told her mother that she was unhappy.'

Sonjoy hesitated a moment, then pulled the letter out of his pocket and handed it to her.

'Oh!' Satya gasped as she read through it. 'Oh my god ... what was the secret?' He took the letter from her gently, replacing it in his pocket. He could guess, somehow, what the terrible secret had been. He took Satya's old, withered hand in his. They were both crying when they got to the hospital.

20

Puja lay white and pale on the hospital bed. Tears were streaking down her cheeks incessantly, although she was in a drug-induced sleep. They had allowed her to wake up a little, but she would not say anything. On Annu's request a friend of hers, a psychologist, had been in to see her. But he pronounced that her trauma was too deep to touch as yet. She would need to be handled, nurtured, with great care before she was ready for actual sessions with a professional. Till then, he would visit her, try and keep her stable, but her actual treatment and hopefully her recovery would start only later. Tosh sat with her. As instructed, an injection had been administered to Tosh to soothe her overwrought nerves and Annu had stayed with her all the time.

The next day Satya gave her the letter to read. Tosh was horrified to learn what this girl had been through. She prayed night and day, through her baths, her meals, her sleep. Praying for her recovery. Praying to be given one more chance at saving this woman, so wounded as a child, so abused. She felt, more and more, that she'd been given a second chance to do something. A chance, a maksad, in life. A mission. She prayed she would get a chance to bring some happiness into Puja's life.

Tosh was sitting by Puja's bed, praying. Their day at the spa seemed aeons ago. She was exhausted, her shoulders hurt and her back ached from a relentless vigil on hospital chairs. Annu had come to relieve her that morning, but Tosh went home just to bathe and change and came right back. In any case, Annu was now in the midst of packing, winding up her job, in the process of leaving the city. Sonjoy had been a gem. And of course, Tosh's friends had been there day and even night, if needed. But eventually, Tosh felt responsible. It shocked her that anyone who had seemed so low, so sunk in despair when she was staying with her, could say these had been the best days of her life. If these were her best, it was unimaginable what the worst had been like. She would make it better. She knew with the help of her friends, she would draw this poor creature out of the depths of despair into which she had sunk and make her bask in the sunshine again. She would. She would.

Sheila and Satya arrived, bringing some hot coffee for Tosh and flowers for Puja. Sheila brought some vibhuti from the Sai Baba Mandir. 'It's to give her strength to recover,' she whispered, slipping it under Puja's pillow. She stirred in her bed. Sheila stepped back, alarmed that she had disturbed her, but Tosh indicated it was all right, Puja was now being allowed to wake up. But then, with a sigh, she slipped back into her stupor. Satya hugged Tosh and held her hand. Tosh indicated they should stand outside in the hall.

Once outside, Tosh sipped the life-saving coffee and had her back gently rubbed by Sheila, who said, 'You know, I have had such a happy marriage. I have only now realized that, after Puja's revelations. Such a happy marriage and such a stable childhood. And to think that I too once felt so unfortunate to have a husband who fell so sick that I had to nurse him in a coma. I thought there was nothing worse. I now realize how fortunate I have been, what a privileged life I've led.'

'I too have been thinking just such a thing,' said Satya. 'Whenever you all talk about your husbands, I always used to curse my kismet and wonder why fate dealt me such a bleak hand. No love, no husband, no family. So alone. But how lonely it must have been for someone like Puja, to have a family, to have a husband and yet ... Surely it is better to be alone and one's own master than to have a person like that to contend with.'

'Husband, I knew, and it is a common story, unfortunate, but common. What I can't imagine is what it must have been like with her father. Beating her so much, do you think it was really that bad?' They all shuddered, it was a terrible, terrible thought. Untenable, unimaginable, unbearable. But it must have been really bad that she could not go back to them after her marriage went bad. That she'd tried to take her own life.

'It is a wonder she did not do this earlier. I've been thinking, I don't think I could have lived if this had happened with me.'

'And that bitch of her mother,' said Tosh with sudden venom. 'How could she have let the husband go on beating their daughter? Why didn't she do something?'

They tried to put themselves in the shoes of the mother, tried to imagine what it must have been like for her, being beaten by a violent husband, seeing your daughter being beaten. And not having the strength, the courage to protest and save the child. The three women were crying and the nurse came up to them with concern writ large on her face, thinking the patient had passed away: the way they were crying, not howling, but still and mournful. They apologized to the nurse who went away muttering under her breath.

'Bitch!' said Tosh with vengeance. They looked at her with amused surprise. 'Arrey, what's got into you, suddenly?'

'Ah, I love the word, it gives me such a kick, such a release, to say it. You should try it sometime when you're really angry.'

'BITCH!' the three said it out loud, ignoring the shocked look from a father carrying his newborn baby to his wife.

Sheila persuaded Tosh to go back to her house. Satya and Sheila would stay with Puja and call if she woke up, if she needed anything. The vigil had really been hard on Tosh; so she allowed herself to be led away.

Sheila went into the room where the only sounds came from the machine that beeped away mechanically at regular intervals. Satya sat quietly reading the Gita. Sheila took the empty flower vase to the bathroom and ran some water into it. Then she brought the flowers into the bathroom, too, and was just arranging them when she heard Puja moan. She rushed back to find her trying to get up, a weak and futile attempt.

'Aunty, Aunty …,' Puja held her hands out, making the glucose drip bottle shake. Satya rushed over to her. 'Yes, beta, it's all right. Don't worry, I'm here.'

'Tosh Aunty …?' Puja looked at her with puzzled eyes, trying to recognize.

'No Puja, it's me, Satya, Tosh behenji's friend?' Satya herself was puzzled; Tosh was not Aunty to Puja, but behenji – they were practically the same age!

'Puja, Tosh behenji has just gone to Sheilaji's house. Look, Sheila is here too. Tell you what, I'll phone her right away and tell her you're awake, theek hai?'

'No, no it – it ... when can I go home?'

'See, I'm dialing, Tosh will just come, she'll take just ten minutes only.'

'No, please don't disturb her. I just ... I just ... wanted ... to say. I just. Sorry. I'm sorry ....' Tears ran down Puja's face again as Satya tried to dial Tosh and reach out for tissues at the same time.

Satya had never been one of those school teachers who could be privy to the confidences of her students. They hardly ever came to her with their problems, but on the few occasions they did, she always felt like a voyeur peeping clandestinely into someone's private life. It made her uncomfortable and she never really knew what to say. However, in the last few weeks – months – with Sheila, she'd learnt to lend a sympathetic ear. So, while she was distinctly uncomfortable, she leaned over Puja, dried her tears inexpertly and told her Tosh was just a phone call away. But Puja was insistent Tosh should not be disturbed. 'I've troubled her, troubled all of you so much, so much. I can't believe that even in this, I've failed. How much I've failed. I can't even kill myself properly ....' She cried, like a child. Helpless.

Satya leaned over her now, wiping the tears. 'There'll be no more talk of killing oneself, do you hear?' She had her school teacher voice on now, she would tolerate no more disobedience. 'It's enough that you tried, thank God He was there to protect you. He was there to protect Tosh. Imagine what she would have gone through had you really managed, if you'd not failed, as you put it.' Sheila, who was hovering near the bed, stood aside now, letting her friend manage. It was better not to crowd Puja now.

'But ... what will I do now, where will I go? I have nowhere to go.'

'You are our responsibility now. Do you think Tosh is in this all by herself? No, you are wrong. We are family to Tosh and we are family to you. You only have to do one thing, promise one thing.'

'What?'

'You have to look after yourself. You have to eat, you have to care for yourself. Can you do that?'

'I don't know ....'

'Eh?'

'I don't ....'

'Say it, promise me that you are going to try. At least promise me that.'

'I ....'

'Yes?'

Puja looked up at the school teacher in front of her. Stern, yet kind; greying, yet sunny, thin as a rake and yet puffed up with concern, a spinster and yet so maternal. She didn't dare disobey this soft, wise matron. She nodded her head.

Satya smiled with relief. 'No, nodding is not good enough. I want you to say it.'

'What?'

'Promise that you are going to try to get better.'

Puja nodded.

'No nodding ....'

'Sorry – yes, I promise. I promise to try to get better, to look after myself.'

'Promise?'

'Promise!'

'God promise?' smiled Satya, her forefinger and thumb pinching her throat, in age-old, juvenile traditions.

'God promise,' said Puja and she smiled for the first time in days, perhaps months, or was it years?

Satya felt as though the sun had burst through on a cloudy day. Sheila came over now and gave them both a hug. This time she grabbed a tissue to wipe Satya's tears. But these were tears of happiness.

When the nurse – along with the doctor – came in to check on the patient, they were delighted to see her sitting up in bed with a slight smile and a tiny hint of colour on her face. When they asked her if she would like to eat something, Puja nodded.

'No nodding ...,' Satya whispered, and like a child, Puja whispered, 'Custard.'

The breakthrough was as much Puja's as it was Satya's. Both had taken a big step, even if – for all the world – the step just translated into asking for a cup of custard.

Tosh – worried at being away for so long, frantic to get back – called Sheila. 'How is she doing?'

'How are *you* doing?'

'I'm fine, I'm coming back. I can't rest here, away from her.'

'Theek hai, if you're coming, then come,' shrugged Sheila nonchalantly, smiling impishly at Puja and Satya, reaching out for the intercom as soon as she'd put the phone down after talking to Tosh. 'Hurry up with the custard, please.'

It arrived just in time. When Tosh arrived, it was to find Satya spooning warm yellow custard into Puja's mouth.

It was going to be all right after all.

Puja progressed slowly, but also surely. Dr Vinod Sabharwal, Sonjoy's psychiatrist friend, was now coming in to see her. But he was worried about what would happen once she was discharged. Having tried to commit suicide once, she could not be allowed to live on her own. Besides, he knew her finances were severely depleted. He talked to Tosh and also had a discussion with Sonjoy and Annu. Tosh said that she'd look after her, but Vinod wasn't sure if Tosh could manage it all on her own. Sheila came in at the tail end of the conversation. Annu actually tried to steer her away with a, 'I'm dying for a cup of coffee, coming Ma?'

But Sheila was too shrewd and replied, 'Yes, I'd love coffee too, right after you tell me what all this khusar-phusar is about.' While Vinod expressed his concerns and doubts, Annu was watching her mother carefully, seeing the thoughts flitting across her face. She could read her like a book. Sure enough, Sheila burst out before Vinod could even finish, 'But I have the perfect solution!'

And so it was that Tosh began moving her own stuff and Puja's into Sheila's spare bedroom even before Puja was told of the plan. Satya was more than happy to shift her things out. After all, she was spending every night in Sheila's bedroom anyway, and there was plenty of cupboard space now that Narenderji's things had been given away. Tosh wanted to keep her own home going as well, of course. For her it was just a temporary move till Puja settled down and they decided what the next step would be. It would be better for Puja not to go back immediately to the house where she'd made the attempt to end her life.

The biddies took turns staying in the hospital with Puja over the next few days. Sometimes Satya, or Sheila or Kunti. Often Tosh, of course. Sheila also needed to spend more and more time with Annu, helping her pack her home up and do some shopping for things she would need there. Annu was naturally worried about leaving her mother with the additional responsibility of Puja Aunty who was in such a delicate frame of mind.

'How will you manage on your own, Ma?'

'I'll manage because I'm not on my own. Look at the way Kunti, Satya and of course Tosh have been caring for Puja, like their own flesh and blood. Look at the miracle Satya pulled off, it was such a sight – to find Puja smiling, eating, I couldn't believe my eyes.'

'But she's still very fragile.'

'Yes, but your friend, your Dr ...'

'Dr Sabharwal – Vinod, yes, he has promised to look after her, treat her. It is likely she'll need medication. It's not going to be an easy process, Ma.'

'I know, but I think we will be all right. I'm glad I'm here. I'm glad I'm being of some use. What good luck we didn't sell the house, that I'm not moving with you to Kolkata. Imagine what we would have done then? I feel I'm wanted here, needed. Really, whatever God does, he does for the best,' said Sheila, repeating one of her most favourite lines ever.

'Now, there's no need to worry. Together we will manage perfectly fine,' she assured Annu.

'But if you don't, if it's getting too difficult, then ....'

'Then what, beta, what shall we do? Of course it's going to have its ups and downs, its difficult days, but what can we do?'

'Ma, you could consider – at least suggest to Tosh Aunty – the option of putting her into an institution.'

'Khabardar!! Don't you dare! This is the first and the last time you will say that. Puja has come to us at a time of her difficulty. Maybe God has sent her to us for His own good reasons. Maybe it is a test, a challenge. Maybe he sent her to look after us, since you had the chance of going to stay with your in-laws. I would never, never dream of putting her away, Annu. Tosh would never do it, that is not the Indian way of doing things. We must look after our own.'

'Yes, Ma, it's just ....'

'Even though she was so obviously depressed, she wrote in her letter she had the happiest time of her life in Tosh's home! Imagine – such a privilege, to give a sad person, a dukhi atma like Puja, some happiness! I consider myself blessed. And so should you.'

Annu hugged her mother then. 'I am blessed, I am blessed to have a mother such as you, Ma. I know that you're going to be all right. You and your ... what do you call yourselves? The BBB's – what does that stand for, by the way?'

Sheila laughed, could she tell her?

'You'll laugh, and of course it is funny, shocking even, but our BBB stands for the Bitchy Biddies Bunch!'

'Oh Ma, you're mad, you all are really mad!' Annu was still laughing when Sonjoy came home.

'What's the joke?' he asked.

'Nothing!!' shrieked Sheila. 'Annu, don't you dare tell him!' She left, in a gale of laughter.

21

Finally, the day dawned when Puja was to come home. Sheila and Satya had gone out to the market and bought all kinds of welcome-home gifts for her, much like Sheila had done for Satya when the latter had moved in. Beautiful little bottles of cosmetics, flowers and freshners, magazines by the bed-side table. Satya embroidred *Puja* twined around with flowers on a bath set that included a big bath towel, a smaller one, a face towel and a hand towel.

Annu, Sonjoy and Tosh went to the hospital to get her. According to the plan, Sheila and Satya waited at a little coffee shop just across the road, in case they were needed or wanted; but basically they would be out of the way in case they were not. They were a bit on edge as well, hoping, praying all would go well. Kunti had gone home, her family had a big get-together.

Puja was subdued on the car ride home. They had told her that they would be staying with Sheila for a while. She had just nodded then and even now didn't seem to notice or care much about anything. Tosh held her hand, but as they approached the house, Puja slid her hand away. She seemed pensive, edgy.

Sonjoy opened the front door, carrying the little suitcase from the hospital and a bag of medication and her discharge papers. The three women followed. Just as she was about to enter the house, Puja stopped, holding onto the door jamb. She paled, seeming to be on the verge of fainting. Annu held her upright.

'I'm, I'm s-s-sorry, I'm terribly sorry ...,' Puja said in a small, shaky voice.

'What, beta, what's happened, don't worry.' Tosh was trying to persuade her to go in.

'Oh Tosh, behenji, I'm so sorry, so sorry. I spoilt it all.'

'You didn't Puja, nothing is spoilt.'

'No, your flowers, your beautiful, beautiful flowers – I spoilt them all. I broke them all. Before … before ….'

The image of her precious flowers lying like broken, mangled dead birds flashed through her head. Why had Puja done it? Tosh had not thought about the flowers once she'd seen Puja lying there. But now she suddenly doubled up with a sense of loss. Of anger almost. Why had Puja taken it out on the gentle, beautiful flowers, blooms that she had nurtured, loved and cared for as though they were children?

'Are you wondering why, Tosh behenji?'

The two women looked at each other. Suddenly a wave of anger the likes of which she had not felt in a long time washed over Tosh. Why *had* Puja taken it out on the flowers?

'Er … why don't we go in and talk?' said Sonjoy.

'No, no, I think I should explain, tell behenji my reason now.'

Sonjoy and Annu exchanged a glance. Why talk of flowers when Puja had come so close to death? But the two older women stood there, at the open door. Puja refused to go in, sensing perhaps that Tosh was angry. She had this urge to explain.

'My father …,' she began, her face twisting with hatred, 'my father loved those flowers. Dahlias were his favourite children.' Her gaze on Tosh was steady. 'He gave more love, more real care to those bloody flowers than he ever gave to me. Or my mother.' She was shaking with remembered hate and fury. 'He'd talk to them, sing to them, make sure they had the correct food, the correct … oh everything, anything. If it was raining, even in the middle of the night, we were made to get up, no matter what. We had to get up and pick the flower pots and bring them in one by one … It was muddy, Mummy was objecting, "don't bring them here, don't spoil the carpets", and he was hitting her, hitting her, telling me, get out, get out there and bring my babies in. And in my mind I was telling him, "But I'm your baby, those are flowers, they're just flowers." But I didn't say anything, I just ran in and out, out into the rain and picked the pots up one by one, putting them onto the carpet, just where my mother didn't want them to be. My nighty was wet through, clinging to me. And when I'd brought all the flower pots in and my mother had been hit enough so she'd gone off and locked her door, my father was looking at me. Looking at me and saying, "Good girl, that's my good girl." And I was so happy, because I knew, for once I knew for sure he was pleased with me, not disappointed anymore. That I'd done the right thing.

'Then he said, "Come inside, come, we'd better get you dry, we'd better get you out of those wet clothes." And I went with him happily and he kissed me, first on the cheeks, then on the mouth, wet, wet and strange. I hated it, I tried to pull away, but he pulled me closer, closer ... I tried to push him, I tried to stop him ....'

Puja collapsed onto the front step, tears streaming down her cheeks from eyes glassed over with remembered grief. Tosh was crying too, unable to take in what was being said. She sat on the lower step holding her, rocking her in her arms. Annu was leaning over the two of them, crouched so that she had her arms around both of them and Sonjoy bent over the three women. Perhaps he was crying as well. From across the street, Sheila and Satya watched this strange montage and wondered whether to go there. But it was a scene so intimate that they couldn't intrude. It was like they were spectators to a silent film.

Puja was far away into her childhood now. She was crying like a child. 'Papa, papa don't please. But he's pulling my wet nighty off me.'

Her arms were up above her head, she'd pushed Tosh and all the others away from her. They watched in horror as she lived through those terrifying moments. Sonjoy reached into his bag to take out the medicine. He wondered whether to call someone, an expert. Vinod.

But Puja was beyond them now. 'The nighty won't come over my head, it's too wet. But he doesn't want my head. He doesn't need my head, my face. I'm stuck, I'm stuck. He holds the nighty up so that my hands are pinned inside, and his other hand starts to roam all over me. "Papa stop, papa don't papa ..." but he won't stop, he's on top of me. He's raping me and my nighty is over my head and I'm so cold, I'm so cold.' She sobbed.

Tosh reached out to her and found her hands were icy, she was trembling, but Tosh wasn't sure whether it was Puja who was trembling or she herself. Puja wrapped her own arms around herself, curling herself into a tight little ball and whimpered words they couldn't make out anymore. Then she lifted her head and looked away, into the house, but beyond them. She was not seeing this house at all, but the long ago, faraway one of her nightmare childhood.

'When he's finished, he pulls the nighty back down, he's stroking me, kissing me, telling me I'm a good girl. I look up and I see my mother standing there. She has seen. She knows. He turns and sees her too. He pushes me away. I want her to hit him, I want her to kill him. For what he has done. But she just moves aside and lets him pass. "Ma ..." "Go to sleep, take a bath and go to sleep." Is all she says, looking at me as if she hates me. She hates me, "but Ma ..."'

Puja suddenly spoke in a sharp voice that was almost not her own. 'Puja! Take a bath and go to sleep.'

Puja stood up now and walked past Tosh, Annu and Sonjoy. They stared after her. Was she here with them or was she still in her childhood nightmare? She turned around to face them, a stony calm over her face.

'It didn't stop after that. I begged Ma, told her we should leave, we could leave, but she slapped me and told me to just keep quiet, that I should stop being so brazen, so batameez in front of him. She said I was a slut, that I paraded myself in front of my own father. That I should be ashamed of myself. The only way for me to stop him was to get married. So I did. But that didn't turn out so well either, did it?'

She sat down on a chair in the living room and held her hand out to Tosh. She was exhausted but calm. 'So you see, behenji, when I saw your dahlias, I just, I don't know. I took out all the anger on them. I can't bear those flowers anymore. They mock me.'

There was nothing more to be said. Puja quietly took the injection that Sonjoy offered. And she went to her room to sleep.

Finally, after Tosh had managed to compose herself, she called Sheila and Satya. They came. Sonjoy called Dr Vinod Sabharwal over as well. It was time for a serious talk.

Vinod revealed that he had suspected the abused childhood. He asked if they would consider putting her into an institution for treatment. 'Seeing that she is alone.'

'She's not alone!' all four women spoke together. 'She's not alone at all, she's got us.'

'I just feel that it is not a good idea for her to go as yet to the house where she tried to take her own life. It is in fact a good thing she destroyed those flowers. It is as if she took some part of the revenge she needed to take. Sort of cathartic, you know.' Tosh nodded, yes, losing her dahlias was certainly worth it if it was going to help Puja.

'But she is too unstable for you to handle it on your own, Aunty,' Vinod said to Tosh.

'Of course, you can stay as long as you like with Satya and me,' said Sheila. 'That would be all right, wouldn't it, Vinod?'

Annu was a little nervous about her mother taking on so much, but everyone else seemed to think it might just be the most perfect short-term solution. Vinod lived close by, so he would be at hand in case he was needed. And there would be the three of them to help with Puja's recovery.

It was decided Puja and Tosh would be in the same room for now.

'Whenever Tosh feels she wants a room to herself, I'll get Annu's room ready.'

'Do you think she'll want to stay that long? Do you think Tosh behenji will agree?'

'Hai, I really wish that they would consider coming and living here permanently, what would be the harm?'

'Harm? I think it would be great!' said Satya, polishing up the brass lamp that stood by the bed.

22

So Satya and Sheila and Tosh began to look after Puja with a missionary zeal. They were like three mother hens caring for one little chick. Sometimes they worried that they were overdoing it. But then, after one of Puja's visits to his clinic, Vinod called Tosh and told her that she was recovering marvelously well. They were obviously doing exactly the right things for her.

Puja herself looked so much better, her eyes finally had some light in them, not the dull stare that they had been quite frightened by initially. She would come into the kitchen to watch Satya at her cooking. Once Satya was making prawn curry – a favourite of Puja's. As always, Puja stood by her, watching, trying to be helpful but without the confidence or courage to take on too much. She watched Satya take the first prawn and beat it gently with the side of a knife, Then she slid the knife along its back and firmly took out the end of the blue vien that ran along its length. She was about to discard the vein into a little bowl when Puja gave a loud 'OH!' Satya almost jumped, 'What, what is it?'

'That vein – why did you take it out?'

'It's a poison. You have to take that out very carefully, one prawn at a time; otherwise we could all be very sick.' She watched Puja uncertainly, as she picked the vein up and laid it out onto the palm of her hand. She examined it very carefully. 'Yes,' Puja said slowly, as though in recognition. 'Yes, it is the poison that spreads. I have a vein just like this one. Right here,' she said, pointing along the right side of her head and down the back of her neck.'

'Pardon?' asked Satya, frightened; she did not know how to deal with this.

'Yes,' said Puja, 'I do, I have this vein. How many, many times, when the pain starts, I imagine that there is someone out there who could make a tiny cut with a very sharp knife – so small, I would hardly feel it, a mosquito bite, that's all. And then, they would take a firm hold of it and pull the poisonous vein out. Once and for all. And I'd never have the pain again. I'd be free of my headaches at last.'

'Headaches? You have headaches?'

'Oh my god, head pains, blinding red pain, that's a better name. Ache means only a little pain. This is a surging red.'

'Red,' repeated Satya, yes, red was what Puja was. Startling against Satya's pale yellowish cream or a sunnish yellow, at best. But Puja was a red.

Suddenly Puja had her by the hand, 'Can you do it?'

'Pardon?'

'You're so good at this. I wish, I wish you could take the vein out.'

Satya was out of her depth now. She herself was so normal, pale, insipid. She didn't know where to begin dealing with this, this – Redness. She'd have to talk to Tosh behenji and tell her of this conversation. Surely that nice doctor Vinod should know.

But just as suddenly Puja changed the subject to coconuts, the one that was being ground to go into the coconut curry, in with the prawns. 'Don't coconuts remind you of beaches?'

'I – I don't know, I've never been to a beach.'

'What? Never? We've got to go, I'll take you one day, theek hai?'

'Sure ...,' mumbled Satya, returning to the comfort of frying onions. Those she could manage. Those she could control.

≈

A few days later Satya was baking, Puja was again at her side, commenting that she could never do anything so difficult. So Satya set her to kneading the dough, rolling it out. Puja loved the feel of the cool, sticky dough between her fingers and even kept a little to play with, after the pastry had been put in to bake! 'I should get you plasticine to play with!' laughed Satya. And the next day, Puja had bought some for herself and they all sat one gleeful afternoon shaping the play-doh into all sorts of things.

'It's like being back in school again!' said Sheila.

'But thank goodness not as a teacher!' laughed Satya, 'I don't want to go back to that again.'

'But I bet you were a very good teacher,' said Puja softly, 'I wish you'd been mine.'

Satya basked in a warm glow all that afternoon. Slowly she realized, slowly, she was turning from a pale yellow, goldening into a honey, warm yellow. No one had ever wanted to be her student. She knew many groaned if they got her as their teacher. Now here, years later, was someone who wanted her as a teacher! And she was a good teacher to her new pupil. She taught her to look out for watchpoints while cooking. 'Just as the onion turns transparent ... when you've reached a dropping consistency ... when it looks toasty, but not brown ....'

23

It was in the midst of one of these cookery lessons that the phone rang. The maid came in with the cordless and announced that the call was for Satya. Satya almost had to sit down in fright. No one ever, ever called her. There was no one who would call her. Besides, her hands were all fishy with the new dish she and Puja were trying out. Puja took over tentatively as Satya rinsed her hands nervously and took the phone with a napkin, so as not to get a fishy smell on it.

'Y-yes?'

'Satyaji?'

The voice at the end seemed even more nervous, more tentative than her's. It was a man's voice.

'Y-y-yes?' the voice was not even familiar. What was a strange man calling her for?

'Satyaji?' He asked again, then there was a long pause that Satya couldn't think how to fill. 'Satyaji, it is me!' There was a triumphant note in the voice and suddenly Satya's mind's eye filled with a creamy, pasty yellow, not unlike her own. It was Gopal Sharma, her downstairs neighbour. But what on earth?

'Sharmaji?'

'Yes, yes,' he was eager, relieved. 'It is I. See, you told me you will keep in touch, but you never. So, so I thought, I found your number, so ....'

'Oh!'

'I hope you don't mind?' The nervousness crept back into his voice.

'No, no, how nice, how kind!' Satya was suddenly suffused with warm pleasure. He had sought her out, found her number. She'd left the forwarding address, of course, but not the number. But he'd sought her out, found it and called her. She wanted to meet him right away. Oh, this was so exciting!

And so it was arranged, Gopal Sharma was going to be the first man who'd be invited to the BBB's and who could imagine that it would be Satya who would be the one to do so?

She was in such a nervous flap Puja finally told her she could manage the muffins and maathis that were to be made. Satya was whisked away to her room by Sheila and Tosh to get her ready. 'Oh, ho,' she protested, blushing, 'it's not a date, bhai, just a lonely old man coming over for a cup of chai.'

'Hain, hain, so where are we saying it's something more than that? But you want to look good for the lonely old man, no?'

But going through her wardrobe, they decided she needed something different, a new look altogether. So, to match a cream blouse, Tosh brought over a cream chiffon sari with little pink rosebuds twining around their green stems. Tosh also got a spray of tiny rosebuds on a silver clip and pinned it onto the slightly off-centre joora and Sheila brought out a double string of pink and white pearls that went with neat tops and a bangle. The bangle was too loose on Satya's wrist, so she was given a watch to wear instead. A little, pretty dress watch, which none of them could use for the dial was so small they couldn't read the time even with their glasses on. A spray of lemony perfume completed the picture and Satya could hardly tear herself away from the mirror. This was Tosh's pastel rose. Pretty, not faded. But when the doorbell rang, Satya's bladder almost let her down. She barely made it to the loo on time. Almost messed up the pretty picture.

He was seated demurely, dwarfed by the big sofa in Sheila's big drawing room. Dwarfed by everything, including his own embarrassment. He sprang as swiftly as his arthritic knees would permit. He was caught between a namaste and a handshake as Satya came in, bearing a tea tray that had been thrust into her hands. Just like a bride. Even if a grey-haired one.

'Sharmaji, how nice, how good of you to come.'

'Nahin, nahin, how good, how good ...,' was all he could manage, his eyes eagerly admiring the newly prettified Satya. She was blushing furiously and was acutely aware her friends were right outside the door.

The only way to cope with these new feelings was to busy herself. So her hands fairly flew about pouring tea, spooning Sugar Free and handing out the cup with trembling hands. His own hands rattled the cup in its saucer. They giggled. A little tea spilled and it made them giggle even more. It was a first date for both of them. Ever. But the spilled tea eased the tension.

'How have you been?' They both asked simultaneously and that set them off again, but this time, the nervous giggles turned to real laughter.

After giving them a little while alone, Tosh and Sheila entered, trailed by Puja beaming over a plate of warm muffins. The conversation was light and easy. Like summer butterflies floating around the room. Pleasant and colourful. Pretty. He was stunned by the deliciousness of the muffins. Swore he'd never had anything quite so tasty in his life. 'My dear, late wife was not a very good cook,' he smiled, mopping up crumbs with a damp finger.

Finally he made to leave. It was a triumph, this visit. One he'd thought of, planned, dreamt and fantasied about. But even in his best fantasies, it hadn't gone off this well. Puja packed some muffins for him to take home. Tosh and Sheila insisted he visit again, soon. And then they left Satya and Gopal alone. Satya walked him to the autorickshaw stand. As he was getting in, Gopal said, 'I have not enjoyed myself for such a long time. I think I always assumed you would be there, upstairs, close by. I never thought of you going away. I – I always thought there would be time. When you left, I was … it was as if … as if …,' he looked at her helplessly. She waited, she was holding her breath, he continued. 'It was as if … I'd lost my last and best chance.'

'Chance?' she thought. What did he mean, what was he getting at?

'I would love to meet you again. I can't ask you home, but would you possibly come to Barista with me sometime?'

'Why yes,' Satya was beaming, blushing, smiling. 'Of course, yes of course I will.'

She wore her dopey smile all the way home and was greeted by peals of laughter and giggles. She flung her arms around Sheila and buried her head into her friend's shoulder. This was beyond her wildest dreams. A date! She! Satya was going out on a date!!!

24

Kunti, meanwhile, had not been around for a while now. Her family was back from another trip and she was busy with them. Her sons had brought her some lovely, lovely gifts. The friends talked to her on the phone and she sounded happy, but she also said that she really missed the BBBs, especially when she heard about Gopal Sharma and Satya. She almost fainted with jealousy and regret for missing it.

One evening she called to find that the four of them, Tosh, Puja, Sheila and Satya were playing rummy. 'Oh, not fair, not fair,' she cried. 'How can you play without me?' She felt a bit annoyed at Puja, who – it seemed – had taken her place with such ease. She knew this was unreasonable and that they were all putting in a lot of effort to help Puja, but she did feel a bit left out.

'Why don't you come here now?' suggested Tosh. On Vinod Sabharwal's suggestion, Tosh's driver was staying in a spare quarter in Sheila's house so that in case of an emergency, they would be mobile. So she suggested she send the car to get Kunti to come and join them. But Kunti was unable to come.

'I tell you, young people nowadays,' she grumbled. 'They're just back from a long holiday, now they've gone out for dinner with friends. Just not content to sit at home and eat simple ghar ka khana, just the family.'

She wasn't very happy staying home to mind the children. They were really big enough to manage alone and she didn't see why she should be the one to be deprived of options.

'Why do you still make yourself so easily available, then?' said Tosh. 'After all, if you're always there and seemingly willing, they can carry on as things are. But if you are not so available, they'll make some other arrangement.'

After she put down the receiver, she told the others of her conversation.

'Suppose she wasn't there, do you think her children would stay at home to look after the young ones?'

'No, but they'd probably get more reliable househelp than they manage with now, simply because Kunti is there to supervise.'

'I really feel bad for her.'

'Oh ho, what's to feel bad, it's just her own grandchildren.'

'I know, but they really treat her a bit like a glorified ayah.'

'Not even that glorified.'

'Best, they should pay her a good salary, and then she'll have nothing to complain about.'

'Haw, how awful, as though they could pay her to be their ayah, what a suggestion.'

'She'd kill her daughters-in-law and her sons for good measure.'

'But at least they'd be paying her something, look how much a good ayah costs these day. And they couldn't find a better person to look after their kids.'

'I heard the Chopras are paying their maid seven thousand rupees now.'

'Go away, of course not, that's too much.'

'Arrey, they've got NRI money, its nothing if you convert it to dollars.'

'But no matter how much you pay, finding good help nowadays is not easy.'

'I tell you, look what happened to Annu.'

'What, I don't know, what?' asked Puja; lately she'd been wanting to be a part of the group, asking about everything.

'She had this really, really nice maid, she was so good, so competent, used to give a lovely head massage.'

'And she used to apply your hair dye also, na?'

'Hai, yes, I had forgotten that. Hai, I hate this in-between stage.' And they all touched their bi-coloured hair where the white roots now outshone the dyed ends.

'So then?'

'Then kya, usual story. She went and fell in love with the neighbour's cook. Annu and Sonjoy came home one day from duty and found her in their bed!'

'Whose bed?'

'Their own, Annu's bed.'

'Cheeeee!' they all shrieked together.

'What a bitch!' shouted Tosh and set everyone else laughing, except Puja who looked rather shocked.

'Oh don't look so serious, bhai, come you can be a part of our group.' And they told her all about the Bitchy Biddies Bunch, promising to induct her into it on the condition that she say the word 'Bitch' out loud.

Puja laughed and giggled, but was unable to get it out.

'No, no, that is the condition, you have to say it. It's a secret club and this is the password. Ok, come on; say it with us first time, theek hai?'

So all together, they came out with one enormous BITCH that shook the foundations of the house.

But an hour later, when they were all in their beds, Kunti called and she was in tears.

'You won't believe what happened.'

'Wait, wait,' said Sheila, putting on her glasses; she always claimed that she couldn't hear without her glasses.

'What's happened?' asked Satya sleepily.

'I don't know, some crisis with Kunti.'

Hearing the phone ring, Tosh also came to their room to find out if all was well. So Sheila put Kunti on the speaker phone so they could all hear what the matter was.

By this time Kunti was sobbing. 'What are you all doing, taking so long?' she snapped at them.

'Nothing, nothing, we are all here. You're on speaker phone, chal bataa, kya hua?'

And Kunti narrated to them the story: she had been watching TV, 'My serial, na? I couldn't miss that.'

'No, why should you miss it?'

'So, just before it started, I was telling the children, "go to sleep, bhai go to sleep. Tomorrow is school." But would they listen?'

'No, of course not,' the others agreed, it was unlikely.

'I even told them, accha take five minutes, then sleep, otherwise I'll call your parents. But do you think they listened?'

'No.'

'So five minutes, ten, twenty, they were still running about, shouting, being such a nuisance. I could hardly concentrate on my serial, couldn't even hear! In the commercial break, again I went and told them, this time even shouted at them and picked up the phone. So they said sorry sorry and went into their rooms.'

'Good, well done.'

'Kya well done, next thing I know, thadaraaaaam! There is a huge crash from Rohan's room. Kya hua? I shouted and ran to see what had happened ... and ...,' she was sobbing again.

'And?' the biddies cried.

'There was Rohan, lying on the floor, blood, blood everywhere. Oh it was terrible.'

This was indeed terrible. 'Is he all right?'

'Ritesh and he were jumping on the bed, Rohan fell off. You know they have these very thick spring mattresses, so he bounced really high and fell straight onto the desk, hitting the corner.'

'Oh no!'

'He seemed to have fainted, baba I got such a fright. He wouldn't answer, wouldn't say anything.'

'Then?'

'I told Ritesh to call his papa-mama. I called the maid. She of course had no idea what was going on, she was watching her TV.'

'Bitch!' muttered Tosh again.

'Anyway, she came, I told her to bring a towel, bring water, I splashed the water on his face, cleaned him up. He revived a little, woke up, started crying as though I had pushed him!'

'Thank God he woke up, though.'

'Yes, thank God, but the bleeding would not stop.'

'You should have put ice.'

'I put ice, baba, I put ice, pressure, but the bleeding would not stop.'

'Then?'

'Then kya, by this time, Ashok and Gayatri arrived.'

'Thank God!'

'Arrey, kya thank God? You should have seen them, shouting, screaming, at the maid. Even ... even ... at me!' she dissolved into tears. 'How much I do, how much care I take, I am an old lady, how much more can I do? Why blame me? As though I pushed him! How much Gayatri screamed at me, that I had been careless, that I should have been more vigilant, instead of watching TV all the time.'

'That's very bad!'

'See, she must have been worried sick, she had to take it out on someone. She didn't mean anything. How is the boy now?' said Tosh, trying to be placatory.

'Didn't mean it my foot, she meant every word, every word, I tell you. I'm not a mother-in-law to her, I'm just a menial.'

'But Kunti, how *is* Rohan?'

'I think it's ok, they've taken him to the hospital, he'll probably need stitches.'

'Do you want me to call Annu?'

'Nahin, nahin, its nothing like that, arrey, don't all of us have stitches on our heads? Childhood is about such injuries. I'm sure it's nothing more. I pray, but I'm really angry, really, really angry at how they behaved with me. No respect, my god, if I ever spoke to my mother-in-law like that ... to bas. Not that I would have, I didn't have the himmat. Just because these women are working, they think they can say anything. And shouting at me in front of the servants. I mean there is a limit, no?'

'Come now, Kunti, you know it's not like that. It must have been such a fright for her to see her son like that.'

'Hain, and you say the other one made the phone call to his parents, who knows what he must have told them, how he must have told them.'

Kunti thought over this, it was very likely Ritesh said some rubbish to his parents just to save his own skin. He was the one who pushed Rohan, so he must have been trying to save himself.

'Two three slaps, these children should get. If Pritamji had been alive, he'd have given it to them with a stick, I tell you. But what can I do? I'm just a helpless widow.'

Now, of course, Kunti would put on the helpless old widow act for all it was worth. But there was truth in her whining. Her children did take a lot of advantage of her. Mostly without even asking her first. It was just assumed she would be there. There had been some occasions, not many, but certainly some, when Kunti had been unable to join them for a spontaneous programme or outing, because she had to mind the children. It really wasn't fair.

'So often I've felt bad for myself, thinking how lucky Kunti is to have her family all around her, whereas mine are so far away, but it's at times like these that I am very grateful I am my own master.'

'I think Kunti's children have brought up their children very badly.'

'They're real brats!' Sheila agreed with Satya.

They offered to come and pick Kunti up, but she naturally wanted to wait and find out how the boy was; besides, there was the other one still to babysit. 'They can shout at me all they want, but when the time comes, they still need to leave their children in my care only,' said Kunti triumphantly before ringing off.

Sleep would not come easily that night. Satya went off into the kitchen, followed by Puja and they made some hot chocolate and got some vanilla biscuits for everyone. They sat in the lounge chatting and then decided to watch some television while they waited for Kunti to call and tell them the news about the boy. The programme they settled on was Wife Swap. Kunti was now the only one who watched the television serials, the saas-bahu ones as they were called. The rest of the BBBs had become conscientious objectors to these. 'The women are made to just cry all the time,' 'Yes, and dress up, full makeup and jewellery all the time, even straight out of bed.' The Biddies had taken a collective decision to put an end to the male sponsored tyranny of the painful aspects of dressing up. No high heels (not that any of them actually wore those anymore), no waxing and upper lip and eye brow threading. They wore their beards, mustaches and caterpillar eyebrows with a newfound pride. Satya and Sheila had even given up wearing bras. So determined to be free were they that they, would put up with the discomfort of bouncing about in the car, rather than be yoked to Maidenform. 'I'm no maiden now, so what do I want the form for?' And of course, they had decided, under oath, 'We're not ready to dye!'

They enjoyed programmes such as Wife Swap. The voyeuristic peek into lives other than theirs gave them a kick. The strange, unrealistic lives on the screen made theirs seem more manageable. In this episode, there was a bunch of children in one household who were complete brats. 'Kunti should see this, maybe she'll learn to love her grandchildren a bit more.'

Puja, now more at ease with them, shyly asked, 'Do they do everything with their swapped husbands? Even ... you know ...?'

It was the first time that any of them had made any sexual reference since they got to know about Puja's traumatic past. It was comforting that she was the one doing it now. It was a good sign, like a wall being torn down. They all sensed this, including Puja herself, as they laughed gleefully at the thought.

'No, I mean, suppose some couple finds that they actually like each other ....'

'Yes, its possible, they may find their swapped husband more interesting, more sexy ....'

'Or wife!'

'Ya, of course, so then?'

'I don't think they'd show that episode, ever!'

'The show would shut down. No husband would like to send his wife for such a thing.'

'Do they sleep in the same bedroom though?'

They'd never thought of that while watching the earlier episodes. But it was a thought full of possibilities.

'Real dirty old women, we're becoming.'

'Well,' said Sheila, 'I don't really care; all I know is that I'm having the time of my life!'

'Yes, I'm having the prime of my life!'

'And I.'

'And I.'

'Me too!'

They all said at once.

'So I say, Balle Balle to us – what say?'

'Balle Balle!' they cheered as the phone finally rang. It was Kunti, Rohan had needed four stitches and was all right. Her daughter-in-law had actually apologized for all the things she'd said in her fright. Kunti was feeling much better, but continued to be more than a little miffed about the whole thing. She was extremely jealous, thinking of the four of them staying up together, chatting, drinking their hot chocolate while she had had to wait alone.

Sheila was the one who suggested that Kunti come over the next day, saying that she should plan to stay the night with them. Kunti agreed readily.

'Maybe I'll come for more than one night,' she suggested.

25

Kunti came with a huge suitcase, as though she planned a long, long stay. Now all the bedrooms in Sheila's sprawling house were filled. Sheila and Satya in one, Tosh and Puja in the guest room and now Kunti in what had been Annu's room.

As had become their tradition now, Kunti's room was also decked up and kitted out with bottles of cosmetics, candles and flowers. She brought along a bottle of whiskey, saying now they should graduate to 'harder stuff.'

The banner was up, the decks of cards and counters in place. The cakes were baked and a new Hritik Roshan film was loaded into the DVD player, ready for them to drool over. Puja had made the most wonderful badges using felt and cardboard and embroidering their BBB logo onto them.

Kunti was, of course, obscenely happy to be here, in the midst of them.

And so it happened that Kunti, with her big suitcase, stayed rather more than the one night. In fact, by and by, she became more of a visitor to her own home, going over when she was invited to join her children, or when they specifically asked her to help looking after the 'brats'.

Tosh would also go back to her own house on occasion. Like when her family came to be with her. Although she brought her grandchildren over for a 'night spend' and they actually loved it.

As Kunti put it, 'Tosh, you and I have one leg in one house and one in the other and we piss on those in between!' The comment, of course, elicited the usual shrieks and feints of embarrassment.

Satya went off for her date with Gopal Sharma at Barista. She had a wonderful couple of hours, this time a little less strained. They found it easier to talk, found that they actually had some things in common. Like the amazing coincidence that they had lived on the same street in Lahore as children! That led to another afternoon a few days later, full of 'remember this and remember that'. They also talked about Gopal's wife. Gopal revealed the strangest thing.

'Do you know, she was really more than a little jealous of you?'

'Of me? Your wife was jealous of me? Why on earth?'

'Well you know, you were a working woman, independent with a salary shalary. Whereas she was housebound. And then, of course, you could drive and even had your own car.'

'Hmm,' was all Satya could say, she was already at a loss for words, even before the big bombshell that Gopal came up with next.

'And then, of course, you were so much more attractive than she ....'

Satya almost choked on her coffee, taking a big scalding sip. In her shock she choked back the disbelief that came instinctively, so he did not realize what a big impact his statement had made. He thought she'd just taken a sip of too-hot coffee and rushed to get a glass of water for her. As she recovered, he said, 'So you see, there were reasons that she wasn't too fond of you.'

Satya was dying for him to bring back the conversation to her being attractive. She kept wishing the others had been there to hear it. No, not only her friends, but her colleagues, her family, her parents. Oh she was singing on top of her voice inside her head. And she was glowing, golden, radiant and – and – ATTRACTIVE! This was just too much. She barely heard what he was saying anymore ....

'So, so what do you think?' his question surprised her out of her golden rush.

'Er – sorry – what?'

'Oh, oh, I'm sorry, I should not have. It wasn't right, forgive me.' He was stuttering, spluttering, spilling. He was a mess as he stood up, almost toppling the chair behind him. 'Forgive me; I'm so sorry, so sorry ....'

She sat there, something important had been said, she had an inkling of what it was about, but not what exactly. But now – now he was getting up, it was slipping away from her. 'I should go,' he gasped.

'Wait,' she cried out, 'wait!'

It turned out that he was leaving Delhi for good. His sons insisted he must come and stay with them in Canada where they were settled. He had already sold the flats and moved to a guest house.

'I just thought, ... I've thought about it so many times. You were just upstairs, so I thought there was always time. But then I was the neighbour, so it was not proper. I am a widower. It will not be proper, but I still thought, I will never forgive myself if I don't even ask.' He was rambling, bumbling on.

He wanted permission to kiss her goodbye. She was shocked. And pleased. She wanted to say yes, but she was also virgin-shy. They walked back to the house. Their hands brushed against each other's.

'Come,' she said at the door, 'come in.' Gentle, for he looked like a startled deer caught in the headlights of a speeding car. She took his hand and drew him into the house. There were kitchen sounds and television sounds. They tiptoed together to Satya and Sheila's room. She pushed open the door. The room was empty. They were sweating sweetly as he closed the door behind him. It should have been an awkward embrace, for she was taller and he was much rounder. But he lay his trusting, balding head on her bony shoulder and she wrapped long arms around him. In fact, they were a perfect fit. They held each other in a comfortingly passionate embrace. And yes, that is how Satya got her first kiss. Coffee and denture flavoured. They held each other close, rocking gently into the other.

'Marry me!' He whispered. 'Come with me to Canada.'

She swayed to a music that came from deep within her. She knew that she did not want to go. She had the life she wanted. The perfect life she'd always yearned for. She'd got her biddies – her closest friends. And now she had just-kissed lips and the arms of a man were wrapped around her.

Right now, at this very moment, she had everything she ever wanted.

'You've completed me ...,' she said, whispering the line from *Jerry Maguire*, a film she and her friends watched and cooed over together. But now she knew what the line meant. She was replete, complete. She gently let him down. He understood. He smiled and kissed her again. But this time it was a goodbye kiss.

As they came out of the door, they were greeted by Sheila, Tosh and Kunti. They stood there looking stunned. A man. Here in their biddy house, coming out of the bedroom with Satya. He seemed to shrink; he actually stepped behind her, hiding, seeking her protection. She stepped back and they were almost shoulder to shoulder, although his were a good few inches below hers. She put her arm around him. 'You've all met Gopalji,' she said, 'we were saying goodbye. He is leaving for Canada.'

They walked out into the night. They knew that the decision she had taken was for the best. And yet she whispered, 'Gopal, I'm so happy, I'm so very happy you told me all you've told me. I'm so pleased we did what we did.'

'Are you, really?'

She looked at him, held him by his shoulders and confessed, 'It was my first.'

She kissed the top of the balding head gently and then they went their separate ways.

26

She came and sat quietly next to Sheila, who took her hand. They were all dying to bombard her with questions. But they knew when to wait.

'He proposed to me,' she confessed. 'He asked me to come to Canada with him.'

AND? Hung in the air.

'Of course I said no. I have all I could ever want here, right here. With you all. I couldn't leave it all. But still, it was nice.'

AND?? They wanted more.

'He kissed me!' She giggled, putting her fingers to her kiss-warmed lips.

'Bitch!!!' Kunti shrieked and threw a pillow at her, spilling the vase of champa flowers.

'Oh, but what a happy, happy bitch I am!'

They burst out laughing. As the laughter subsided, Puja, who had not said a word till then, now whispered a soft 'Bitch'.

They looked at her with astonished delight, Tosh hugged her. She was now one of them completely.

A contented silence descended. Each one looked back on the hand life had dealt them – the pairs, the rotten full hands. And now there was no regret, no rancour. Just a deep sense of fulfillment.

The next morning, Sheila called a sign painter and had the nameplate changed.

She didn't tell anyone about it, just asked them all to come out. And there, read the new signpost:

PURE SEQUENCE

They stood outside the gate. Their gate, holding their hands aloft – fingers linked in loyal bonds – and shouted at the tops of their voices – BITCH!!!

And then they went back into their home.